Patricia Kavanagh

Wire Me to the Moon

MARGARET DOLAN

POOLBEG

Acknowledgements

To Captain MacDermott and crew of Poolbeg, especially its leading light, Kate Cruise O'Brien, thanks.

To the Arts Council and Aer Lingus for my flight of fancy.

Published 1997
by Poolbeg Press Ltd
123 Baldoyle Industrial Estate
Dublin 13, Ireland

© Margaret Dolan 1997

The moral right of the author has been asserted.

The Publishers gratefully acknowledge the support of The Arts Council.

A catalogue record for this book is available from the British Library.

ISBN 1 85371 772 X

Cover illustration by David Axtell
Cover design by Poolbeg Group Services Ltd
Set by Poolbeg Group Services Ltd in Goudy 11.5/14.5
Printed by The Guernsey Press Ltd,
Vale, Guernsey, Channel Islands.

For

Freda Gavin

About the Author

Margaret Dolan was born in Dublin and now lives in Ratoath, Co Meath. She works as a freelance journalist and playwright. She has won both the Francis MacManus Award and the Powers Short Story Competition. Her first novel, *Nessa*, was published in 1994 by Poolbeg.

Contents

Wire Me to the Moon

*T*his morning sun entered my body. It came streaming in through the window, through the blinds in gold bars, spreading hope, wrapping me in its warm glow.

When the sun hit the prism, colours spiralled around me as if I was inside a spinning top. Rainbow colours. Happy colours. I hugged myself with the unbearable thrill of being alive.

After the operation, after they sliced off half my left breast, I was immersed in a maelstrom of turbulent dark and malevolent colours swirling around inside me. Muddy browns and maroons, greens and purples. Mostly the colour purple. One big purple pain scorching through my body on a scream.

For a while I drifted on a grey fog of drugs keeping the pain at bay. But even then a huge blot of yellow, cowardice yellow, would whoosh through me. Terrifying me into childhood prayers. If I'd been X-rayed at that time my whole inside would have been one great big splodge of cowardly yellow.

But right now, at this very minute on this light and upbeat golden day, I'm pure gold. The sun has entered my body and I have the Midas touch . . .

I want to spread the news, spread the good word. Tell Jean.

One day, one ordinary day, you wake and there it is. Surprise, surprise. Waiting to be discovered. Fright creeps up your neck like a hot hand. Your eyes run down your face to the spot. Not wanting to see what your fingers feel. A cluster, like spring bulbs or seeds that bump up the earth ready to burst through. Only these are not expected, not sown by me. The Judas kiss of cancer planted in my breast.

Mastectomy skitters around my head in lumps. Lump, tumour, growth. A lump by any other name . . . oh God . . . oh God . . .

A month after the operation when the wound had healed I was wired up. Through my left breast . . . New treatment . . . sealing, killing off cells.

"Wire me to the moon," I say half laughing to the young nurse. She half laughed too.

"I could light up like a Christmas tree," I say.

Blue, radioactive stuff pumped through my breast on wires. To gobble up aspiring lumps. Emptying my left breast.

I want Jean. I want my sister more than anything else. If she knew, she would drop everything and fly half way round the world to be with me. That's why I didn't tell her.

I want to tell someone, though, anyone and everyone what it was like. Especially Cora.

Cora who doesn't want to know. Cora who wants to know everything else . . .

Cora who has pinned me to the cabbages beside the

4

deep freeze in the supermarket extracting information from me. Gossip. Information I didn't want to give. Shouldn't have given.

Hurtful sad information. I, the only one with the information.

I held back the news from Breda and Nora but I told Cora Malone.

The three of them, Cora, Breda and Nora, were off playing golf and missed the drama of the runaway wife.

Breda and Nora came the following day sniffing around with their cream cake and sly looks. Hunting information. Asking questions. They knew she had flown. There had been talk. It had been expected. Her wings had been flapping for some time. But they were truly miffed to miss the flight. And on their own doorstep too.

Did she time it deliberately to vex them? No, she wouldn't have given them a thought.

So, having missed the big picture, they came for the details. The nitty. I made coffee.

"You must have seen," they said ". . . the afternoon . . . you always garden in the afternoon."

I could feel the tic in my right eye racing with lies as I denied seeing what I had seen. From the herbaceous border I witnessed Sonia Kennedy leaving her husband and watched him literally crawl down the path after her begging, beseeching. Saw her jump into her lover's jeep and zoom away. Her pony tail bobbing. I was the only on-the-spot witness apart from their three little blonde girls.

"Get up, get up," the eldest, ten-year-old Florence,

ordered her father in her mother's clipped tone. "You're making an exhibition of yourself." The middle child said nothing, just rolled her hands into tiny fists. The youngest sucked her thumb vigorously.

Cora got me in the supermarket between the cabbages and the deep freeze cornering me with her trolley. I still said I saw nothing . . . then after much interrogating I said nothing-much . . .

And then, with my knee hopping with held-back information and my eye ticking, she extracted every single bit from me. Bits I didn't remember seeing . . . The whole bloody scene like a scab lifting. The humiliating scene with poor Peter begging on his knees.

And I felt guilty and miserable. So much so I began bringing around cakes and things to the Kennedy family and offering to help. Peter was mortified. Looked away. The eldest resented me being a witness too. The middle one didn't seem to care and the little one slid her hand in mine and her little warm hand made me want to cry. I didn't let them down any more but it didn't change anything. I had betrayed them to the mob. Held their pain up to ridicule. Gave it to Cora beside the cabbages in the supermarket. She glowed, hardly able to contain herself. She had it straight from the eejit's mouth. She could hold forth in the golf club. Holding every eye and ear with each juicy morsel. Embroidering as well of course. Maybe even have the jeep running over his fingers and, by the time the story left the club, Peter would be in intensive care with multiple injuries.

I knew it wouldn't get back to him. He didn't go out

anymore. Better if it did. He could accuse me. I could admit, apologise, ask forgiveness. What he couldn't forgive me for was being there, witnessing.

When the removal van came and went, they drove after it without looking at me in my herbaceous border, except for a tiny wave from the little one. I felt justly punished.

Cora seldom cornered me after that in the supermarket, I was no use to her. Except as a listener to her aches and pains. She told me about her hysterectomy, from diagnosis to operation to after-effects. Every stitch. The lot. Nobody had suffered like she had. And everyone, just everyone, said how brave she was. Even got a holiday in Barbados for her bravery.

The nurses said I was brave. "A model of courage" they said. I wasn't, of course. But I grabbed the lie anyway and held on to it. I was afraid, afraid of death but mostly afraid of pain. I wanted them to knock me out, anaesthetise me, stuff me full of pain-killers and valium. Or at least hit me on the head with a mallet.

"A little tug and that'll be it. Won't feel a thing . . . Well, maybe a teeny tiny prick like a prick of a needle," the doctor said.

Nobody thought the wires would stick. That the flesh would grow over them. I didn't want to be there in my blue radioactive room, in my senses, watching and feeling the wires stick.

"Get a grip," the doctor says when I start to whimper. I can see his dandruff . . . smell his breath, his sweat.

"Good girl," he says when I stop.

He pulls. I want to scream my pain to the world. A tiny little moan sneaks out of the corner of my mouth.

"You're not helping," he says.

Helping? Helping whom? He who said I didn't need a local anaesthetic. He who hasn't got a breast with lumps and wires stuck through it. He who doesn't care, wants to pull the wire out of me with my flesh attached. He who now says I'm not helping. He pulls hard.

This guinea pig squeals long and loud and full of pain. Showing him up. He wants to slap me. I want to kick him to death.

"SISSSSS" . . . involuntarily waters through the nurses' teeth as they watch.

When the wires came out, harbouring bits of my flesh, he couldn't look me in the eye. Sister gave me pain killers and brandy and I slept and slept.

The whistle blows. I've got it. The all clear. They've let me out. I want to howl it to the skies. Or at least from the bean-stack in the supermarket. I want to stand on the pile of bean tins and scream, "I'm all right. They've taken it away."

Along with bits of me of course.

Breda, Nora and Cora are in the supermarket . . . They see me coming. Pushing my trolley. Breda nudges Nora at the wines and nods in my direction. Surprised I am alive and well and shopping. Embarrassed. Probably informed the golf club the neighbourhood spinster had IT, the big C . . . and whispered, "it's only a matter of time."

Breda is preparing to bolt with her wire basket.

"How-are-you," she shouts on the hoof as I wheel

8

my trolley towards her, dashing past before I can say "Fine, I'm fine" or better still – "Rumours of my death have been greatly exaggerated – " But she has gone.

"How is everything?" Nora asks when I catch up with her at confectionery. Eyes fastened on the cream doughnuts.

"Examine yourself," I say sowing the seeds of fear, "it's everywhere."

She takes off, scalded by my words. God forgive me but I'm glad, really glad. Cora actually abandoned her groceries and left the supermarket rather than meet me. Nobody wants to press me up against the freezer and extract the details from me. The word is enough to make them run for cover. I don't need a leper's bell. If I'd had a bypass they'd have come around, settled down, made themselves comfortable wanting to know everything. Ask about the veins. Ask to see the wound. Asked about the diet. Counted the stitches. Might even have visited me in hospital. But they don't want to know about my mastectomy. I wanted to tell them about that. I want to be told again I was a model of courage. I wanted to tell them, Breda, Nora and Cora, the wires didn't come out clean. They stuck, like a chicken on a rotisserie. Bits of flesh, my flesh, left on the wires. I wanted to tell Cora especially. To pin her to the deep freeze, watch her turn green. Unburden myself. Offload my pain. Freeze her blood.

Through the glass doors I watch Cora running scared across the carpark. Tomorrow, or the next day, I'll follow her here. Ram her trolley, stick her to the freezer and tell her everything. Everything she doesn't want to hear.

The sky is blue. Hopeful blue and the sun is shining. I can't wait to feel its warmth again treacling through me.

I'll write and tell Jean. Start with the Midas touch and go on from there.

Oh look . . . there's a butterfly!

Animal, Vegetable, Mineral

❖

*Y*ellow, hazy yellow, fills my eyes.

Darkness edges in and clouds my eyes, my head, my mind. Black, coal black, blots the scene enveloping the yellow and all of me.

Glued lids tear apart. Yellow, bright yellow, floats in. Daffodils, yellow daffodils, dance in a vase. Drooping lids flutter open and close under black pressure. Again plummeting into pitch black.

Crusted lids creak open. Yellow, yellow, tinged with brown. Wilting daffodils hang their heads. Dead. Am I dead too? Shadows pass on tiptoe. Voices hushed and reverent. Medicine bottles clink. Blackness suddenly swoops down sucking me into darkness.

Eyelids open in slits. White light hurts my eyes. Nothing but white light. I don't seem to have a body. No hands, fingers, feet, toes. I'm just a head. A dead head and I've arrived somewhere. But where? Where would a fullblown atheist arrive?

Hell, Heaven, Purgatory, Limbo? Has to be Limbo. Limbless in Limbo. As a child, I always imagined Limbo as silent white light with unbaptised dead babies floating around. Then Limbo was abolished. Must have reopened it for the atheists. Silent white light. Nothing for all eternity. You believe in nothing, so nothing you get. I wish I'd had the time to formulate an afterlife theory of some kind or stayed agnostic. Hedged my bets.

My head seems to be stuck sideways. And there's something up my nose and it's not my finger. Well I presume it's not as I don't seem to have any. I can hear noises off. Out of sync. Humming. Voices.

Scarred, rheumy eyes zoom into mine, out of clay-coloured wrinkled skin.

God? Couldn't be. Couldn't look like that. Anyway Limbo is supposed to be a place where you never see the face of God. The ultimate punishment. Or is that Hell?

Must be another inmate. Another dead head.

The mouth opens wide. It emits a high-pitched scream. The scream catches in mine and we wail in unison. Another head pushes into view. Coarse ugly face.

"What ails ye, Peggy Brown?"

"The cabbage," she says, pointing at me.

Cabbage! Me a cabbage? Reincarnation! I never thought of that. But how could anyone be reincarnated as a head of cabbage? A cow or a pig, but a head of cabbage! Maybe it's because I'm a vegetarian. We are what we eat and all that. Am I today's dinner? That'd be a real, here-today-gone-tomorrow reincarnation.

"Its eyes are open."

"Just because its eyes are open doesn't mean anything. Can open automatic like or else it's the end. Last fling, everything works, then out like a light. Better off out of its misery if ye ask me. Lying there two months vegetating. Taking up a bed. Easy know it's not a public patient."

I'm alive! In hospital, two months. My legs must be sprouting.

"What'll we do, Kathleen?"

"I don't know about you, but I'm going home. I'm finished."

"Ah but Kathleen, we better tell someone. Can't leave her unattended if she's dying."

"Go on then, press the emergency button and be ready to go or we'll miss the bus."

Peggy's face swings into mine gusting bad breath. "The nurse'll be here in a minute, love, don't fret."

"She better be. CIE waits for nobody!"

"Ah sure we're not in any hurry."

"That's neither here nor there. We're in our own time, unpaid."

They have moved out of my line of vision but I can feel Kathleen's annoyance in whatever she's jiggling.

Shoes squeak.

A new voice, breathless, asks, "What's up, Kathleen?"

"It's the patient, Nurse Keogh, her eyes opened and we didn't like to leave the poor misfortunate, even though our shift is over."

A face, young and fresh with perfect eyebrows, looms into mine.

"Hello Shirley, how are you?"

Fine, I'm fine.

My ears aren't working properly or my voice is weak. I can't hear myself talk.

A frown flitters across the face. The face disappears.

"Peggy, you hold the drip, Kathleen round the other side and when I say lift, lift. Right, lift, mind the drip, raise the back-rest, good, now ease her back, that's it. Thanks."

I am on my back. Propped up.

"There you are, Shirley, a room with a view," the nurse says, panting.

I can see out the window. A garden. A tree.

"Can you hear me, Shirley?"

Yes of course I hear you. But I can't hear myself. The old vocals must be rusty. Bound to be. Out of action for two whole months. *Y-e-s n-u-r-s-e.* I push the words, Sisyphus-like, up the hill from my larynx, only to slide back down again without an utterance. Not even a gurgle. I have no voice. I have gone from verbal diaorrhea to muteness in two months.

"Get Mr Smith, Peggy, he's next door."

"Certainly, nurse."

Peggy clatters off, while Kathleen drums her fingers on the windowsill.

"Not looking good, Kathleen," Nurse Keogh says.

"Buggered, if you ask me," she says, looking out the window.

Thank you, Kathleen, for that.

"Ah shite, there's the bus turning."

"If you hurry you might still catch it."

"You must be joking. Anyway, might as well wait for the verdict."

"Clear the room, nurse," the doctor booms as he sweeps through the door, followed by Peggy.

"Kathleen, Peggy . . . " Nurse Keogh says.

"That's the thanks we get for lifting private patients in our own time. Come on Peggy," Kathleen says sashaying out.

Peggy tiptoes behind her, hiding in the larger shadow.

"Arousal from persistent vegetative state to what?" the doctor muses. "Let us see. If you understand me, Shirley, raise your right hand."

I can't. I don't know where it is.

"Raise your right hand if you understand me?"

"Not a flicker. Can't detect a glimmer of consciousness in the thought process. Out of *PVS* to severely disabled. Oh dear, oh dear, what an impoverished quality of life. We'll give her physio and some medication to stimulate. We can but try. No matter how good we are we can't recreate a brain."

Hey, hey, wait a minute, you pompous fart. Look at me. I can see, hear, think. My eyes must show something. A glimmer even?

He writes on my chart. A two minute diagnosis. I wish I could spit. A nice big gollier between his bulging dirty grey eyes.

"She's dribbling, wipe her mouth, nurse," he says and goes.

They come and go. I come and go. In and out of light and dark. I fight the black monster that sucks me in and spits me out at will.

I'm turfed out of the darkness into the wee small hours before the milky light of morning. A lot of people die around this time. Read it somewhere. Fragile time. Body at its lowest ebb, waiting for the cold grey dawn or the grim reaper. God was smart. Got me in my own time. I can just imagine him saying in a Humphrey Bogart accent, "So sweetheart, you don't believe in the hereafter! Well Shirley baby, I'll let you have your hell in the here-and-now, with plenty of time for reflection. Here's looking at you, kid."

Mum called me after Shirley Temple. My wild curls tamed into ringlets. My feet trapped in white buckskin boots. My sister Diana the same. We were hauled around the country to competitions. Medals clinking on our chests. I rebelled. Ran away. Dad put his foot down. Hadn't to sing or dance for anyone anymore. Now I can't do either. Do anything. Didn't even get to run away. Stopped in my tracks. Struck down in the right place, at the right time. Legs defuzzed, in my new silk undies. Lot's poor wife got it in the neck for just looking back. I got it for my wicked intentions. Still, I can't imagine God poking his finger through the clouds and saying "Peter, get that scarlet woman in the fancy knickers." Hardly his style.

I wish I could remember what happened. I remember the day. I remember writing. I can see the notepaper, cream vellum and words in blue ink throbbing and the pain in my head bursting psychedelic all over the place. Words falling off the page. And then nothing till I landed up here. Shirley Tyrell the head. The only bit of me working and nobody knows.

Tears are falling from my eyes. I can feel them running down my face. I wish I could die. Curl up and die. But I can't even curl. I can feel the darkness coming, black hole sucking me in. I hope this is it. The big bang.

I'm awake again.

I had a dream. A nice dream. I am dancing and singing "The Good Ship Lollipop". Mum is telling me I'm better than Shirley Temple.

Today the room is sunshine yellow. Glowing. The hawthorn tree is in full flower.

It is so beautiful I can almost smell it. It must be May. May is the month of Mary. May devotions. May altars. Why am I thinking like this? Have I been converted while I slept? Maybe I'm doing a Saint Paul. From Saul to Paul, from Shirley to Pirley. God knows what happened in the last months. There I go again, God on my mind.

Nurse Keogh and another are plaiting my hair.

"Hope she doesn't nod off again. Terrible anticlimax. The family milling around and she lying in her finery like sleeping beauty."

"It's all the same, asleep or awake."

"I suppose eyes opening after two months isn't much but still, it would be nice for them to see her awake. A bit of hope."

"There's nothing there, Mr Smith said and he should know."

"Just because you've the hots for him doesn't make him infallible. I heard of a case . . . ."

"I'm not going to argue."

"Touched a raw nerve have we?"

"Shut up Fitz."

"Sorry. The husband's a bit of all right, wouldn't throw him out of bed for farting."

"Yeah, a fine hunk. Imagine being left with your woman. Could last twenty years."

A life sentence. My life whittled down to waking and sleeping. Even my voice swept away.

"Terrible tragedy. Good looking woman too. Massive hair."

"Bramble bush," Nurse Keogh says, roughly tugging.

Ouch! no need for that.

"That plait's too tight, all the little hairs are caught," Fitz says.

"It'll do," Keogh says, pulling the hair at my temple.

AAaahh.

"Jesus, Maura! A tear. She must feel . . . "

"Does it all the time."

"All the same, I'm going to loosen it up." She does.

Thank you, thank you.

"Hello Shirley," Kevin says shyly. Mum bunching in behind him. And Diana gushes in on an enormous smile.

Poor Kevin. He's not wearing his serve-you-right, you-runaway-you look. Of course it has been two months. Maybe he's forgiven me. But he hasn't got that, even-though-you-done-me-wrong I forgive you, look, either. Poor innocent, handsome, boring, Kevin. If only I could remember. Poor Mum. All that awful pink powder. It's catching in my throat.

"She's awake, fourth time lucky," Diana says leaning over me.

Now that I've been reduced to ears, eyes and nose, I am acutely aware of every look, cadence and smell.

I can smell Diana twice, her skin and her perfume, separately. Mam, stale face powder and stale talcum powder. Kevin, tobacco and what? Sweetness, innocence?

20

"Pure silk! What good taste you have, Kevin," Diana is saying, fondling my nightdress.

"Sorry?"

"Shirley's clobber, I presume it was you, hardly your mother's taste."

"Shirley herself actually, nightdresses, negligees, the lot."

Poor Kevin, blushes like a schoolboy. I fell in love with the hairs on the back of his neck. Nineteen eighty, Trinity College, Dublin.

"Silk! All silk lingerie?" Diana squeals.

"Yep, must have had a premonition. You know she even had her case packed."

"Yes, yes, I know that and the note and all, but what I'm saying is, 'Dear Kevin, I've packed my bags', doesn't tell us anything. I mean, pure silk!"

"It tells us how thoughtful she was. Always thinking of others."

"I wonder who she was thinking of when she packed these goodies."

"What are you implying, Diana?" Mum says, glaring at her. She'd like to slap her face.

"All I'm saying is, they're more like dirty weekend clothes than, 'Oh dear, I'm having a brain haemorrhage, I'd better pack my case so as not to inconvenience anyone'," she snorts.

"Diana!" Mum warns.

"Sorry, only joking, Mum, Kevin."

You shit-stirring bitch, Diana. Some things never change.

"No offence taken. Sure Shirley and I are a bit long in the tooth to go on such weekends," Kevin says.

"Dead right, Kevin," Diana says, smothering an expletive. "Your mother on her way?"

"No, can't come, sends her . . . "

"Nora can't come! Only yesterday she was elbowing us out of the way, armed with her relics, claiming Shirley's awakening as her own personal miracle."

Kevin is uncomfortable. Embarrassed. "Actually she broke her denture as she was coming out the door."

"False teeth! Nora has false teeth, I'm gobsmacked. Mum was always saying what fine big teeth Nora had, weren't you Mum?"

"Indeed , they were so, so natural." Mum deliberately not looking at Diana.

What big lies you tell, Mum.

A knock on the door. Everyone looks, anticipating. Nurse Keogh peeps in.

"Mr Smith would like a word," she tells Kevin.

Kevin squeezes my hand and leaves. Strange sensation, watching someone squeeze your hand and feel nothing. Then again, haven't felt anything for years.

"Don't know how I kept my face straight," Diana guffaws.

"Clickety click, the worst fitting dentures I've ever seen."

"Shirley would have enjoyed that," Diana says.

I did. I did.

"The poor lamb, I blame that aul vegetarian stuff," Mum says, shaking her head.

"What?"

"I don't care what anyone says, I'm sure it was that aul vegetarian stuff that brought this on."

"Eating vegetables turns you into a vegetable? Don't talk rot, Mother."

"Shush Diana, what'll Shirley think."

"She's not thinking. Look at her. She looks great but her face is blank. She's not even aware we're here."

"I refuse to believe that."

Kevin drags in, slowly, sadly. Idly takes my hand. The sympathetic head tilt tells me I'm fucked.

"What'd he say?"

"Irreversible damage." His big wounded eyes, damp.

Oh Kevin, lovely Kevin. Shy, naive, solid, reliable. All the things I had chosen him for then, and was leaving him for, two months ago. I wish I'd finished that letter, releasing him. And Johnny. What about Johnny? Another fine mess. Another hour and I'd have been his burden. What would he have done? Leave me on a hospital doorstep and creep away?

I close my eyes and hope they'll go.

"Ah she's asleep. Better make tracks," Diana says. Dying to get away.

"Need a lift, Diana?"

"No thanks, I'll take Mum."

"OK. And Carmel, when you see mother . . . "

"My lips are sealed," Mum says wearily. All the stuffing knocked out of her.

I drift into sleep. I break out of my cocoon. I communicate with my eyes. Eyes right means yes. Eyes left means no. The nurses fuss. The doctors applaud. "Didn't she do well," they marvel.

I awake to slate grey drizzle. It doesn't dampen my spirit. Today will be my day. Today I'll show them. I practise. Left a bit . . . Right a bit . . . Left a bit . . . Right a bit. Morning clatters in. I'm so excited. My big breakthrough.

"Hello, Shirley," Nurse Keogh says absently, taking my pulse.

Look at me, I scream in silent black despair. She doesn't.

The physiotherapist, she'll see. I wait for hours. She comes. She pumps my dead limbs up and down, chattering away. She doesn't even look at my face.

They feed my body and exercise my limbs and starve my brain. Inside my loglike body I scream and rant and rage. And they see nothing.

In my previous life I should have joined The Right To Die movement. Left a living will. Turn off everything. Do not resuscitate.

Again I'm sucked into darkness. I'm glad. I want to go in and not come out. I want to die. Faces from nowhere, from everywhere. Diana screaming at me. But I can't make out what she's saying. Kevin stroking my cheek. Mum pontificating and then I see his face. My lover's smiling face. Johnny's face. His love reaches into the darkness of my mind. I smile warmly. I cry with joy.

"How are you, my little cabbage?" he says. "Nothing to say? Not even a word of apology for standing me up? Having stood outside Bewley's for six weeks, I said to myself, Shirley must have missed the bus. Then I thought, sure she's always late, so I waited another fortnight, but alas! This your excuse? Come, come Shirley, you can do better than that. Leaving me standing in the rain in Grafton Street while you slept. Not good enough. What have you to say for yourself? Still refusing to talk? Sulking? OK, OK, so I was lying when I said I'd wait forever but . . . "

He is fading, fading. Don't go . . . Johnny, oh Johnny. Voices and faces and noises and smells jumble and crowd my mind. And I'm plummeting through time and space clawing my way out of my tomb. How long have I been there, hours, days? My hair is wet with despair.

I smell freesias. Freesias. My favourite flower. A huge vase of freesias perfumes the room. Did I dream Johnny? Which came first, the freesias or Johnny? Did the smell of freesias spark off the dream or did he bring the freesias? He always gave me freesias.

We met at a poetry reading. I saw him but did not take notice till he spoke. His rich, burnt voice enhanced his witty, clever conversation. I tried dipping my gaze from his lined, lived-in face, cracking like cement as he laughed, but couldn't. He waved his cigarette like a magic wand. And wham. I went gooey with love.

Next day I reviewed our meeting, savouring again every word he had spoken in that burnt voice. Reconstructed his face. Every line accounted for. And he rang and asked me out. I expected sparklers from my fingertips.

Saturated with happiness, my earsplitting smile flowed ahead of me. Unquenchable. In my heightened condition I loved everyone. Even the most unlovable of my pupils.

Diana said whatever I was taking, she wanted some. At the school they thought I was pregnant at last. Kevin said he never saw me so happy. He had suggested the poetry reading when he saw I was getting restless. Always suggesting things to do, places to go. Keep me his.

And when Johnny said let's take Paris, I said, *yes, yes, yes.*

Mum, Kevin or Diana do not refer to the freesias. They have brought flowers of their own. Red roses from Kevin.

Another day. I don't know if it's the next day. Sometimes I think I miss whole days. Another smell. Horrible. It's catching my breath. Musty. I open my eyes a little. I snap them shut. It's Nora and her relics.

"Poor Kevin didn't deserve this," Nora mutters.

Dead right, missus.

"He never should have married you. Flighty. All that wild hair. I warned him about marrying an older woman."

I am two weeks older than him, seven weeks and two days to be precise, you old cow.

"And not a chick or child."

Whoa there, that's not . . .

"And now this. Hopefully this relic will send you on your way."

Amen I say to that. I want your lethal mercy.

"Oh God take this barren woman . . ."

26

"You're breaching the trade descriptions act, Nora Tyrell."

My eyes fly open. Mum is standing there glowering at Nora.

"What?" Nora is flustered.

"You were feeding God misinformation. Our Shirley is fertile. And that's a fact."

"I didn't . . . " And by the look on her face, she didn't. "I was trying to help her with my relics."

"Oh yeah? Trying to wipe her off the face of the earth, more like. Lucky for you God isn't open to offers and if you don't want to be handed to him on a plate yourself, you better stop offering Shirley, OK?"

"But Carmel, it's for her own good, she's not much more than a vegetable or won't ever be. A lively girl like that, trapped. It would be a blessed relief," Nora says in her concerned voice, but she is nervously gathering her bits together.

"That's a matter of opinion," Mum says moving closer, deliberately knocking her bulky frame against her. Terrifying her.

Nora takes flight.

"And another thing, Nora Tyrell, those germ-laden dentures of yours should carry a health warning."

Nora's mouth opens and closes like a goldfish as she scuttles out. Mum laughing like a drain. Oh Mum, you are cruel but then so is Nora.

"Don't fret, love, I'll take care of you."

Oh fuck, I'm going to be Mum's cross. Pity Nora didn't put a pillow over my face.

I'll be the cleanest, shiniest, best dressed invalid

wheeled out for the neighbours to coo at, spray spittle into my face as she accosts them with my tragic saga, embroidering as she goes. Telling them how the shock nearly killed her. How I heroically tried to write to Kevin. My writing all higgledy-piggledy. Receiving Extreme Unction and all the trimmings. Looking forward to my first words. My first steps. They, marvelling at her, taking on a spastic who can only dribble. I'll be Ireland's first atheist saint. And she'll make me wear a bloody great dribbler.

Sparrows in the tree twittering the day into life. Life! I wish I could extinguish mine. But I can't even do that. I've tried holding my breath but my mouth always bursts open.

Hang on, I think I feel . . . I do feel . . .

Aaah! My toes spreadeagling in cramp. A cramp in my left foot. A delicious awful, wonderful cramp in my foot.

Thank you God. Oh, thank you God.

God?

Well, yes. I suppose.

28

Curiosity and Cyclones

❖

*C*hristine watches the trains coming and going, disappearing, sucked like worms into the bowels of the tunnel till their tail lights are no more than fireflies. And coming. First a halo of light growing, frilling at the edges, burping out of the tunnel dragging a chain-gang of graffiti-covered carriages whose sides open neat as a cut throat, pouring people out in a liquid frenzy on to the platform. Then, with a sigh, she and others are sucked in and propelled at breakneck speed under the ground to be spat out at stations along the way. Standing, jammed upright, pressed by sweating bodies, eyes grazing the curved sides, she imagines she is in the belly of a whale but mostly she feels she's riding a cyclone.

The day had such possibilities. New Docs. A full blown sun riding the New York sky. But by St Mark's the stiff new leather has gnawed her left heel. The thought of taking off her new boots and standing on their cold floor keeps her throbbing along in the heat, crepe soles sucking the sidewalk. By the time she limps into Tenth Street and the corner of Avenue B, it is raw. And she is locked out.

Unlacing her boots in a honey pool of sticky afternoon sun, she feels his little beady eyes on her. Creeping over the stoop, resting on her frayed jeans. Fraying her nerves. Arresting her fingers. She pushes her eyes sideways till they hurt and catches the still profile of a man on the adjoining stoop, spread fat and melting.

She whips off the first boot. The second sticks fast to her blistered heel. Gritting her teeth she gives a short sharp tug and with a wet plop the boot comes, seeping pus through her sock and tears through her closed eyes. Pain everywhere, spreading meanness and viciousness. Just let him move an inch, she mutters tying the boots together. Swinging them like weapons.

Time slugs on. If only Terry or any of them would come. She rakes through her mind. Nobody said, don't come Tuesday or Tuesday is a bad day. She'd have remembered.

Christine's father left on a Tuesday. Pancake Tuesday. Just a week after adding an extra brick to keep out the O'Reillys.

She waits at the gate. The warm buttery smell of pancakes tinged with lemon floats out every time her mother opens the door.

"Any sign?" she says stretching her eyes over the tied gate. And Christine shakes her head.

Cold and darkness drive her in eventually. The gas is turned off and the cold pancakes shrivel in congealed butter. Christine nibbles an edge but all she tastes is bitter lemon.

"Must have got delayed," her mother says, puffing her cigarette nervily.

Next day the priest stabs her forehead with ashes.

"Thou art dust and into dust thou shalt return," he says and tiny particles of dust float on to Christine's eyelids. She wants to turn to dust there and then.

"He'll be back," her mother repeats. The bullet-grey thumb print marking her faith. The light grey cigarette ash catching in the threads of her jumper.

"Never manage without his precious trains."

But Christine has seen the gaps. Only tracks and carriages left. He had taken his prize possessions, the engines, and left her with the replaceable. She kicks and smashes urged on by the thwack of splintered tracks.

Wordlessly her mother sweeps up the debris and returns the room to a bedroom and takes in Spanish students.

Kids fly high on swings, in the park opposite. O'Reilly's great swing fills her mind. A huge thick rope knotted at the end slung from a mighty oak. All the pals came and sat on the knot and shooshed into the unknown, bellowing Tarzan cries.

"Try it," Billy O'Reilly says sitting on the dividing wall, "it's deadly, like riding a cyclone."

Cyclone . . . she rolls the new word around her tongue.

"Get down before she sees you," she warns as her mother's words, "Keep away from those bloody O'Reillys" skitters through her head.

Billy laughs. He's not afraid of her mother. Not even a teeny bit. When she was younger she was terrified of him and all the O'Reillys.

"Curiosity killed the cat," her mother used to say when she caught her peeping over the wall into their back garden. It was a great relief when, at the age of nine, she discovered none of the O'Reillys were called Curiosity or killed cats. At the age of ten she was more afraid of her mother than of all the O'Reillys. She wanted to be one of them. Jump on the Tarzan and soar through the sky, maybe even fly over a rainbow.

"Go on, ask, tell her I'll mind you," Billy urged.

"Cyclone! I'll give him cyclone," her mother said and made her father add another brick to the wall.

Christine had her own little swing made of hairy scraggy rope. Short and whiplash tight. Stop her landing on the flower bed or worse still fly over the wall, escape.

"What's a cyclone?" she asks her father.

"It's a, it's eh, look it up in the dictionary," he says.

Christine couldn't find a word starting with a sigh so he finds it for her.

– Cyclone, a violent hurricane of limited diameter – the dictionary said.

Years later Christine rode her own cyclone out of Ireland, landing in Manhattan pursued by a whirlwind of motherly whines and accusations. She didn't feel guilty, she felt free. Now that her mother is buried in the cold wet clay in Ireland, guilt does come into it.

She feels her predator moving in. She looks stoically ahead.

"Hot today, like some refreshments?"

She turns and looks. Can't help herself. His face is putty coloured, threads of hair, seconded from side growth, are meticulously tracked across his bald dome, bubbling with sweat. Shirt buttons strain and a maroon tie chokes his neck. People run from men like him. Didn't he know?

"I've everything laid on. My place," he says jerking his head at the house behind him.

She shakes her head, swinging the boots ominously.

"No offence," he says backing off.

She wills them to come. Flopping on her bony wrist the gold needles of her watch point to three o'clock. She'd give them five more minutes. He's hardly going to manhandle her into the house or anything, she tells herself, flattening her rising panic. Wasn't it daylight and all the kids around and everything.

"I've the whole house, only me. The chapel's in the attic."

Oh my God! a religious freak. All those tears in my jeans. And that patch on my bum, a scarlet patch. A scarlet woman, a Jezebel. Kill me for my sins.

She holds her trembling lips still with little inside bites. A blood-curdling screech quivers the air. A little kid howls, holding tight to the chains of a swing, refusing to budge. Kicking. Pigtails stiff with temper. Her perfect caramel skin turning blue as her mouth slams shut.

"We gotta go now, Darlene honey, Mommy will bring you again tomorrow," her mother coaxes.

The child doesn't budge or let out a breath.

"No respect, children have no respect," the fat man tuts.

"Honour thy father and thy mother," he yells across at the child.

The child's mouth opens letting in air. Her face returns to caramel. Her eyes huge.

"Go fuck yourself," the woman screams back.

"Did you hear that?" the man asks, eyes bulging, neck growing like a squeezed red balloon. "Unfit, unfit to have children."

Cupping his mouth he roars, "A tree is known by the fruit it bears. A mouth speaks what the heart is full of. Your words will be used to judge you."

A quick wrench separates Darlene from the swing. The woman hauls the startled kid away, giving the fat man the finger. The little kid, aping her mother, holds up one tiny finger.

The sweat bubbling on the fat man's head bursts and trickles down his face.

Like a sprinter on a starting block, Christine is about to take off when she sees Terry, sun-spangled in black and gold, scything through the park on his blades. Dreadlocks flapping, earrings swinging, gliding towards her. She smiles. The fat man intercepts the smile and beams back. She lets him. Terry has arrived.

"Yo sister," Terry says crunching to a stop.

She expects smoke from his wheels. People stare.

"El diablo," a Hispanic whispers, blessing himself.

A coarse chin nuzzles Christine's neck, making her jump.

"How's she cuttin'," a voice, thick and creamy, says as Frank's face, surrounded by blond curls like pencil shavings, bobs upside down into her own.

She laughs. The fat man slaps over in monk's sandals.

"Howdy neighbour, John Smith junior, at your service," he says, extending his hand. "Call me Junior."

Junior is at least sixty-five.

"My daddy is eighty-six," he says to the unasked question. Terry shakes the proffered hand, introducing Christine and Frank. Christine barely touches the fat fingers. Junior invites them over for refreshments. Christine tries to give Terry her no-way look but he's taking off his skates and accepting.

"I'm not going," she whispers to Frank. "I'm afraid."

"I'll protect you."

"Oh yeah! Like when that juicehead stuck the gun in my neck and you were out of sight so fast I thought I'd imagined you were with me?"

"Didn't I bring the cops?"

"When I was already robbed and could have been killed."

"Terry, slayer of dragons, will take care of you and I'll run for the cops, OK?" he says, his Harpo curls dancing.

Terry, she supposes, could give Junior a few well-chosen chops from his Aikido range if necessary. So, barefoot, she too follows the flat slap of Junior's sandals.

The heavy door groans open revealing a blackened gutted interior where the only things standing are a rickety staircase and steel girders holding up the first floor. The whole house is on a slippery slope, listing to the left.

"What happened here, man?" Terry asks.

"A fire, long ago. Never got fixed up. Except my place at the top."

"Is it safe?" Terry asks, testing the stairs that tilt drunkenly from the blistered wall towards the matchstick rail.

"Sound," Junior says, shaking the skinny rail bannister almost to destruction.

Christine spikes Terry and Frank with her eyes. They shrug. Junior trudges onward and upward holding the lean rail which sags and waves under his weight.

Come away, come away, Christine wants to shout, imagining the fall and jellied thud. "Come on up," Junior wheezes, from the first landing.

Clinging like burrs to the charred flaking wall, Terry and Frank follow, trailing their curiosity behind them. Christine inches along, nails digging deep into the blackened rail in vertigo desperation. Long dirty windows on each landing let in murky light.

38

Breathless and panting, they reach the top floor.

"How come it's empty?" Frank rasps.

"Whole building about to be gentrified," Junior says, unlocking a heavy oak door.

A sumptuous feast lies before them on a long table set for twelve, they look at it and at each other, incredulous.

"Sit down, sit down, no, not there, Christine, there, opposite the mural, you there, Terry and Frank here," Junior orders, pointing.

Christine sits strangling her hands under the table. Goosepimples big as marbles bump through the gaps in her jeans as she looks at the mural of the last supper and reads the writing on the wall. "Many are called but few are chosen."

The chilly premonition implodes in a tidal shifting inside her and she feels the full weight of her fear as his beady eyes creep over her to the jagged jeans.

"Wow! Look at that," Terry says, eyes impaled on the wall behind her.

Frank looks and whitens.

Christine twists her head. Eyes, cats' eyes, green and glassy, stare back. Dead cats. A whole shelf of them. Stuffed.

"There's more than one way to skin a cat," Junior says.

And all three men crack up laughing.

A scream, dormant in Christine's throat, bursts, piercing the air as she jumps up and runs. Bare feet flying. The scream carries her down the rickety stairs, wailing off the peeling walls, out into the street. Drying into a cough in the hot parched air.

Barefoot, she picks her way to the subway to be gratefully swooped up into a carriage and sucked into the womb of the tunnel.

Her mother had been right all along. Curiosity kills cats. And he's everywhere.

Damaged Goods

I have stopped the words seeping through the radio speakers. Zinging on the telephone wires. But I can't stop the written word coming sleight of hand through the letter box. So I wait. Every day I stand in the hall waiting. Waiting for the postman. I watch him coming through the stained glass. Blurred blue and red and green. All colours. But I still jump. My heart slews across my chest when the letters hit the floor. Fear particles floating in the sunbeam. The letters always fall written side down.

Today his fingers dug into the soft fat parcel as he squeezed it through the letterbox. I was expecting it. My Punjabi apron. Free gift, six tokens. I put it on. Lately it has been brochures. Thick brown envelopes plonking down. All addressed to Aidan. I don't touch them. My anniversary surprise, foreign holiday, somewhere exotic.

"Nothing but the best," Aidan says. Twenty-fifth anniversary next week. The cake is made. Our initials – AA – entwined in silver bells. AA! and the two of us Pioneers. Two dry sticks. Plenty of room for Aidan and Alice.

He's a good man, Aidan. I never wanted for anything, good provider, never a row, a black and white man. He loves me, my black and white man. He loves the person he thinks I am.

Words will change all that. Words shrieking along the telephone lines, pouring out of the radio, concealed in white envelopes. The phone, the postman and the radio all conspiring. Voices and words accusing. I have to stop them. Stop them upsetting Aidan. When he leaves the house, I sneak up on the radio and pull the plug. Nudge the phone out of its cradle and wait for the fingers in the letter box. I want to slice them off. Watch them drop one by one into the hall.

Yesterday was a bad day. Really bad. I even forgot the gravy. It's here beside me on the hall table. Thick-skinned glutted gravy, congealed to the brim in the fat-bellied sauce boat, Aidan's mother's. If I pierce the skin will it run like blood from an open wound?

No one said. Not one of them said "Where's the gravy?" Not even Paul, my younger son, who loves his gravy. If anyone asked, I'd have remembered. I know I would.

The trouble started that morning with Peter, my older son.

"Mam, I'm moving in with Ann," he said as he left for work. Just like that. My heart was beating like a kettledrum. Bursting through my skin. As the words were leaving Peter's lips, I was concocting a story. A story to tell Aidan. A lie. I was always like that, even as a child, thinking on my feet. Saving my skin. Sly, my mother said.

"Don't tell your father. You know he doesn't approve of co-habiting."

44

"Ah Mam, you can't go on shielding him from life. I'm not ashamed of what I'm doing and I'm not going to lie about it. It'll do him good, get him out of that time-warp."

"But, but . . . "

"Lookit Mam, is he suffering from some life-threatening disease that a bit of exposure to the real world will finish him off?"

"No, of course not. Just a bit black and white, but a good husband, a good father."

"Yeah yeah, I know all that, you've been using it as a weapon all my life, keeping me in line. As a child I was afraid to do anything wrong in case I'd upset Da and he'd drop dead. It was a terrible burden, Dad's goodness."

"I didn't realise."

"If he's that fragile that he can't cope with his twenty-four-year-old son moving in with his girlfriend, that's his problem. You know Ma, real life stops at our hall door. Limbo. We're in Limbo presided over by Aidan the good. Tyrannically controlling the television even. If you don't watch it, your creation will stagnate in his own righteousness."

Is that what I've done to Aidan? My gratitude preserving him in bigotry. Had I told him, had I confessed that day in November, would he be a more compassionate man today? Would he have grown? Those hard lines softening, blurring like running mascara. Or would he have run away? I was afraid to take the risk. I never meant. Too late now.

So I'm standing in the hall in my Punjabi apron with the glutted gravy. The gravy nobody asked for. The

45

phone distracted me. Screeching at me as I carried the gravy to the dining-room. I had to stop it. I put the gravy down on the hall table and grabbed it. Holding it down, stopping the words. Stopping the words hissing out of it. Accusing me. But it wouldn't stop, kept clanging away, words boiling over the edges zinging through my finger tips. Peter came up behind me and undid my fingers one by one, releasing it. It was for him. His friend Mark. I went into the dining-room.

And instead of saying, "Where's the gravy?" Aidan said, "Who's on the phone?"

"Mark," I said.

Peter came in grinning.

"Guess what? Ciara's got her first tooth."

"Ciara?" Aidan asked.

"Ye know Da, Jenny's baby. Pass the spuds, Paul . . . ta."

"Mark's some tulip lumbered with that one and someone else's bastard."

Bastard whipped across the table stinging me like a wet dishcloth.

"Jenny's a single parent and the baby's not a bastard," Peter said evenly.

"Boils down to the same thing."

"What's it to you? Mark loves Jenny and the baby and he's prepared to support – " Peter snapped.

"Support!" sniggered Aidan. "On what may I ask, his dole? Parasites living off the state. It's *us*, the taxpayers who are supporting . . . "

"You bloody hypocrite," shouted Peter, "out there with your placard of a mutilated foetus, preaching the sanctity of life. All right to protect the unborn at *no* cost, is that it?"

"They should be taken and given to respectable married couples."

"Taken, why not go a step further, herd the mothers into concentration camps and brand them so they can't contaminate Irish family values."

"They are already branded. You can always spot damaged goods."

"Maaam," beseeched Peter, "what do you think?"

I said nothing.

"Come on Mam, surely you've some opinion?" Peter coaxed. "Don't be afraid, you're allowed have an opinion, isn't that right Dad?"

"Of course, speak up, Alice."

I remained silent.

"Afraid to upset Dad, is that it?"

"You won't be upset, will you Da?"

"Of course not, we've been married almost twenty-five years and have no secrets. Fire away, Alice."

"Dad has given you permission to speak the truth, the whole truth and nothing but the truth, so what do you really think, Mam?"

I didn't answer. Afraid. I was always afraid. Born afraid, a ten month baby afraid to come out of the womb knowing I was already rejected.

"Is that the best you could do?" my father said when I was born. My mother told me often, passing the blame. I, the fifth disappointment following my four sisters. Lucky for us, Da got it right and number six was a boy. Lucky for Mam. He went on a binge. My brother John brought light to our lives. Mam called him her prince. Saviour more like. Number seven was another boy. Mam really relaxed then. Done her bit.

We girls ventured out of the shadows. John was so welcome we all benefited. When Patrick came, we even laughed out loud. Da's cronies said he should go for the hat-trick but he decided to hang up his hat.

"No point in tempting fate," he said. He was sixty and all stomach. Mam was forty-seven.

He ignored the boys same as us but boasted about them in the pub. "Two fine sons," he'd say and sometimes add, "and five skirts." Mam spoilt the boys and so did we. Of our own accord. We kissed and hugged them till Da said we were overdoing it, making sissies of them. He wanted strong young bucks who could swing a hurley and take care of themselves. They were as rough and tough as he'd wanted. Macho men.

"Maaam . . . " Peter says desperately.

Aidan sees my silence as solidarity and preens. I want to hit him between his eyes with the truth. A wail started in my womb. An overpowering keen like when Paul was born. Great big gulping sobs stream from me. Paul jumps up and holds me in his arms.

"Look what you've done to your mother," Aidan accuses.

"Meee, what *I've* done. Look to the mote in your own eye, mate," Peter hurls back.

The last time I cried out loud was the day Paul was born. As I cradled him in my arms this terrible animal cry burst from me. I rocked and hugged him and wept. Crying for my lost child, Aisling, weaver of dreams. My little red-haired love child. Matt's child. Nobody asked me why I was crying. They gave me an injection and I stopped.

I was a raw little country girl bewitched by Dublin. To me it was Hollywood. "Alice in Wonderland," Matt used to tease. Matt smooth and handsome as a film star. I literally went weak at the knees every time I saw him. Twenty-eight he was and knew everything. Sent me flowers. Wined and dined me and brought me to the theatre. Imagine! Just like in the pictures. No wonder I fell head over heels. My friends called him Mr Wonderful. Eileen, my sister, called him flawless. He even bought me an evening dress. It was the most beautiful dress I'd ever seen. Pale green, frothy and drifting like gossamer. He gave it to me for my eighteenth birthday to go with my red hair. Same time as he gave me the baby. Disappeared when I told him I was pregnant. Eileen said I should go to England and get rid of it. But I was sure Matt would come back, armed with flowers, begging my forgiveness like the chap always did in the movies.

Sick every morning, I lost a stone. My legs were like matchsticks. Friends thought it was because I was pining for Matt and tried to bring me out of myself. My bump didn't show for six months. Then only slightly. The vomiting had stopped and I began to look better. Everyone said the bit of weight suited me. At eight months I took the boat to England. Alone. And three weeks later had a little red-haired girl in Liverpool. Called her Aisling. Came back and gave her away.

The nuns said they'd find a good home for her. I nightmared about my little red-haired baby. Always crying out to me. Arms outstretched like the Famine children. I was afraid to go to bed.

At weekends I looked through the bars of the orphanage. Terrified I might see her. I never went in. I sent presents instead. Guilt making them bigger and bigger. Did she get them? Did the nuns think she was getting too much and withhold them? I began to hate the nuns, blame them.

I was an extra virgin when I met Matt. Untouched. Not even kissed. Unable to gauge love. The realisation that he didn't care destroyed me and I abandoned my baby.

I saw him once, soon after, in Grafton Street. Having scanned me for signs of child-bearing, he came towards me, his charming smile pasted to his lips. I smiled encouragement. Then spat my revulsion into his handsome face and watched the glob of saliva slide down his cheek.

I stopped loitering outside the orphanage. I wrote letters instead, asking about her wellbeing, her whereabouts. And never posted them. Continued sending presents with love from Mammy.

Eileen suggested we go to New York. I didn't care where I was so I agreed. We waitressed. I sent presents to Aisling. Eileen married a New York cop whose granny came from Ireland and I came back to Dublin and got a job as secretary to an accountant.

The day Aisling was three years old, I made so many mistakes my boss chided me. Three years. Tears flowed. The poor man sent me home in a taxi apologising for being a brute. Next day he was so contrite I nearly told him about the baby. Instead I said I'd redo yesterday's work. And closed off my past.

I married him a year later. I didn't mention Aisling. I covered my tracks well, not a crumb. I keep telling myself Aisling was adopted by loving people who doted on her. Who knows, maybe it's even true. She's frozen in my mind at the age of three. When I see a vulnerable little child sitting on the cold grey concrete, begging, the whole bloody unhealed wound erupts, making me want to howl to the world – Give me back my baby –

Aidan and Peter are into home truths. Aidan white and tight. They have forgotten about me. Paul holds me gently. Peter's shouting about real life. Aidan's at the "Get out and don't darken my door again". Peter says that suits him fine and he'll move in with Ann. That really upsets Aidan.

Paul says, "Who are we to judge anyone, can we afford to throw stones?"

And Aidan says he could and would. I want to shout, you can start stoning me.

But I couldn't do it. Not to Aidan. Not in front of the lads. Especially after what he said, damaged goods and all that. I couldn't let my sin, buried in layers like a cultured pearl, burst over the table like pus from an overripe wound. So I postponed contaminating the family. And my stoning. Peter left blaming me. Said I fed Aidan's bigotry. An insult to women.

So, I stand here in my lovely Punjabi apron beside the gravy. No letter seeping with sadness. The phone stifled.

Maybe at this very moment Aisling's telling it on the radio, crying on the frightened air encouraged by the chat-show host. The presents sent with love from Mammy. Even from America. Remembering her fourth

51

birthday when nothing came. Aisling, with her red hair and freckles, smiling desperately. Not pretty enough, unwanted, left with the nuns.

The last time Eileen was home I tried to talk about Aisling.

"You should have done what I suggested at the time," she said, "had the abortion, like I did, it's easier."

I never knew.

Poor Aidan. I did him a terrible injustice. He deserved a virgin. Living with damaged goods for twenty-five years. Lose his street cred, as Peter would say. Bad tree, bad fruit. Someone to blame for Peter moving in with Ann.

I hate November, season of twists and hollow truthfulness and anniversaries and weeping earth. She was born in November. Today actually. Twenty-nine years ago today.

I don't think Aisling could find me. I covered my tracks well. More than likely not even looking. Probably celebrating with her own family. Not thinking about me. She might have children of her own. Maybe even a little red-haired girl. I hope she isn't thinking about me, spoiling her birthday.

No need to tell Aidan. Not yet. No point upsetting him. He's a good man. A black and white man, but a good man. I could meet her secretly. Tell her my dilemma. Explain about Aidan. She probably isn't even looking. Maybe I could, you know, inquire discreetly. I'd have to leave if he found out. Couldn't bear the way he'd look at me. "You can always spot them, see it in their eyes, brazen," he said, looking me straight in the face.

Poor Aidan. Poor Aisling.

A Foggy Day

❖

"Cornflakes or porridge, Missus?" asks the new ward-maid throwing me into confusion. My listomaniac, tea-leaved and programmed-for-groceries mind, whirls through porridge, cornflakes, milk, sugar, sausages, eggs, butter, tea, coffee, bread . . .

At bread my mind clicks to John and the whole bloody scene cracks open. I'm standing at the door. The pink flowered door of the squat in London. Brown bricked and ugly lurking behind a dusty hedge riotiously out of control and snagged with sweet papers and veils of translucant plastic bags blowing in the wind. The punk plumed in orange and purple is sitting on the step.

The house, the punk and I are misfits on this street. I want to run but my big feet won't budge.

Nerve ends wave in terror as I try to burrow deeper into the thick duvet of grey but the fog keeps thinning . . . thinning . . .

"Porridge or cornflakes?"

The words scrape and tear through my cocoon, leaking the grey until it becomes a destitute sieve. Holes threaded together. Through the biggest hole, I see roast beef and knives and forks and prawns and souffles and a tin opener which brutally prises the lid off my mind exposing me to the last dinner.

I am confronted with the meal which started the row, which led to the flight that landed me here in a lunatic asylum. Of course it's not called a lunatic asylum, something more refined. But I bet the locals call us lunatics.

I have lain in a grey wordless fog for ages. Weeks, months, whatever. Not a word since I arrived. Just the odd whimper when the slate spume boiled red with fury. Set alight by hatred of Ben, my husband. Extinguished by needles puncturing my skin. Spreading greyness. Sucking me deep into soft puffy nothingness. Happy in the slow creeping mummification of my emotions.

Now my cosy cocoon is pierced by choice. Porridge or cornflakes.

Until today no one asked. Just left either one.

"Hurry up Missus, I haven't all day."

I point to the cornflakes, shake my head and point to the porridge then the cornflakes again. She'd like to do me an injury. Sighing, she sort of slings the bowl. I watch it twirl and zing and settle. I'm fully awake. Choosing cornflakes. Remembering everything.

Had Colette, my brother-in-law's wife, not had her face and bum lifted and her bosom filled with silicone, I wouldn't have been at that house on that day and probably wouldn't have lost my mind. I didn't feel mad or anything. Giddy and a bit giggly – except for my feet which were immensely sensible as only size seven and a half can be. Looking back, the cochineal in my hair was screaming madness. Poor me thought it was crying freedom.

It started with Colette. No, it was Ben, letching after Colette's silicone. No, I must get it right, it was Ben's brother Mike, husband to the vamp Colette, who started it.

Ben and I were standing at the door, bidding Colette and Mike fond farewells, when Mike kissed my hand saying, "That was a beautiful meal Nora, you are indeed a Cordon Bleu cook, you do everything so well."

Ben chimed in slimily, "And what do you do well, Colette?"

I can't remember her exact reply but it was said in her usual husky tone with all the sexual connotations. My little bit of praise was turned into a testimonial to sexpot Colette.

"Isn't Colette something else," Ben continued in bed as if plain people like me had no feelings. "Has the secret of eternal youth."

"Yes, she used to be two years older than me, now she's two years younger. At the rate she's subtracting it'll soon be ten."

"She can afford to pretend with her looks."

"No chain marks on her legs from being fettered to the kitchen sink."

"Couldn't tie a bird like that down."

"Not like me."

"You're a home bird."

"Never wanted to be, always wanted to roam, see everything, do everything."

"You wouldn't survive in the big world. Colette was born to travel."

57

"Maybe if I had my face and bum lifted, my varicose veins drained, my hair strawberried blond and silicone implants, Mike would covet me, like you covet your brother's wife. I'd have culinary advantage."

"Nora! I never . . . how could you . . . I'm very disappointed in you," he said wounded.

"Is that so? How very obtuse of me not to have noticed."

"I hope you haven't said anything to Colette."

"Don't have to, she answers your vibes all on her owneo."

"You do me a grave injustice."

He turned his back in a black sulk, taking most of the duvet, and fell asleep muttering. I lay there despising the person I had become.

Had my brain perished from lack of use? How did I let that snoring heap belittle me, stamp on my dreams? I could leave. I could leave.

"I'm leaving," I say out loud, shocking myself. Ben stirred, snorting in his sleep. Whimpered when I chucked the duvet from his greedy gammon hand. Trembling with excitement and fear I sat up. I, who even in my dreams couldn't get further than the end of the road without turning back, was leaving. *Leaving*. I kept saying it softly, hushed, like it was a miraculous word . . . like it could spirit me away.

I thought of John, my younger son, who was always trying to motivate me.

"Shift yourself Ma, or you'll be found fossilised to the kitchen sink," he'd say. "Don't you want to see places, spread your wings?"

"I do, I do. But you know your father."

"Go it alone."

I'd never been anywhere, not even a package tour to Spain. Ben didn't like the heat so I trailed behind him to the West of Ireland every year. God I was an eejit.

Could I take off on stubby broken wings like an escaped battery hen? The awesome agoraphobic excitement of it all left me breathless. What if I was a failed runaway and had to crawl home, begging forgiveness, asking to be taken back?

He'd take me back all right, to satisfy his greedy gut if nothing else. The thought of him drooling, snouting at the cooker, sniffing for pudding decided me. Never again, I'd rather become a baglady. I'd start in London and go on from there. Tibet, I always fancied Tibet. I drifted asleep on the magic word *Leaving*.

When I refused to get up and make his breakfast, Ben showered me with abuse. Didn't ask was I sick or anything, just banged around in the kitchen. The smell of burning toast wafting like incense, cemented my decision.

My going away outfit consisted of a low cut shrunken T-shirt, John's discarded bondage trousers and denim jacket. I tightened my bra straps, hauled up my sagging breasts and left them perilously tethering on the edge. My lank hair was lying flat on my head so I back-combed it adding a good dash of cochineal. That was a mistake. I left a note with plenty of food for thought and none to eat. Took money from our joint account, a plane to London and landed on John's doorstep.

Only it wasn't John's anymore.

"Lookin' for someone, darlin'?" asked the purple plumed punk sitting on the step, his chains rattling and clanging.

"Yes, John Fallon."

"He doesn't live here any more."

My heart jammed. Then pumped viciously around my chest.

"Where is he?"

"America, gone to preach."

"Preach what?"

"The good word."

"What good word?"

"I dunno, do I?"

"A born-again?"

"Get off, only in it for the bread, isn't he, and gettin' it buttered on both sides. TV preacher, that's where the money is."

"He couldn't, doesn't, he wouldn't even look the part."

"He does now, all collared and tied and suited. The blond hair's cool, a real golden boy, our John."

"But his head's shaven except for the squiggly green and pink bit at the back."

"Ever heard of a wig, darlin'?" He paused. "I was to go with him but I wasn't ready. Couldn't compromise, after gettin' me image together like, know what I mean?"

I nodded, looking at the Sharons, Glorias and Michelles trellising up his arms encased in hearts and pierced by arrows.

"When will he be back?"

He shrugged. "I dunno, could be back already. Like I

said, John doesn't live here any more. Has a new pad in yuppie land with Miranda."

"Siobhan, where's Siobhan?"

"I dunno, musta given her the push, has this dish Miranda, Miranda the celibate chic." His cockscomb swayed with laughter.

"Are you sure it's John Fallon you're talking about?"

"Oh yeah, John Thomas Fallon."

"But he's an atheist."

"What's that to do with anything? He's only doing it for the bread. Manna from heaven he calls it."

"I thought he was helping the deprived."

"The depraved, darlin'. The monied depraved. American thickos who want to book a ticket to heaven and John is selling."

"Have you his new address?"

He hesitated. "Not on me but his brother and cousin will be back soon. John gave them the squat when he moved out."

"James and Andrew?"

"The very ones. Demolition workers. Pulled down half of London, most of it intentionally." He laughed and slid away.

I sat until I was numb right through while the words – John doesn't live here anymore – slipped and sloshed around my head. John defected . . . one of *Them.* Siobhan the vegan replaced by Miranda. Great shoals of blood gushed round my head, fizzing my ears. Making me dizzy. I'm going to have a stroke I thought, on a whoosh of panic. Get a grip, I told myself, trying to stem the fear seeping through my body. But still it came and still it grew till my stomach was awash with foreboding. Before my last carrier bag of courage left me I deflected my thoughts to Colette. I imagined myself snipping the stitches behind her ears and gleefully watching her jaw drop. And then letting her boobs down like the air out of a tyre. This cheered me immensely until I remembered silicone doesn't deflate.

James and the punk panted at the gate.

"Mother?" James queried, hoping I was a figment of his imagination.

"James!" I said, amazing myself with my clipped practical voice.

"You OK?"

"Yes, thank you, James. Why?"

"You look . . . different."

"I'm making a statement."

He sat down cautiously beside me.

"What sort of statement?" trying to stop the sneer clogging the words.

"Surely you can see the significence of my gear?"

"You look like a tube of toothpaste with the lid left off, topped by a burst red biro and that's only the half of it."

"I wouldn't expect you to understand, that's why I came to John. Remember his speeches about us being slaves of society?"

"I remember them well."

"Well, I'm following in his footsteps. His disciple."

"What's that red shit dripping down your face?"

"Cochineal?"

"Sorry?"

"Food colouring, when I decided to spike my hair it looked so drab I decided to give it a lift."

"It's not really you, is it Ma?"

"I don't know what you mean."

"Your feet are a dead giveaway. What has Dad to say about all this?"

"I left a note, didn't describe my runaway gear."

"Your what?"

"I've run away, left a note with a few well-chosen expletives. I should have fucked off years ago."

His head jerked as if I'd hit him.

"Mother, what's got into you?"

"I've seen the light. Found God out. You know, Jesus sent poor Martha back to the kitchen with a flea in her ear while the lazy bitch Mary chatted him up. Imagine poor old Martha slaving away while Mary enjoyed the craic and gorged the food with total approval of Himself."

"We all have our calling," he said sanctimoniously.

"I've never heard of anyone called to the kitchen sink."

"Not in so many words."

Looking at him I could see Ben. In a few years he'd be snoring in front of the telly, drooling pools into his spare tyre.

"If you want to be John's disciple you'll want to change your image pretty sharpish. Your son John is a preacher. Does a God spot on American television," He said with relish.

"So I hear but I find it hard to believe."

"Believe, Mother, it's true and he's making mega-bucks."

63

"And you and Andrew into demolition? Strange occupation for a sociologist and a psychologist."

"Strange but rewarding, we too make loadsa money. Actually we're in the process of buying this place," he said, getting up.

As he was putting the key in the door, Andrew arrived wearing a forewarned look.

"Auntie Nora," the cheeriness almost reaching his eyes, "what brings you here?"

"Colette, I'm doing a Colette, looking after the blessed trinity, me, myself and I."

"My mother is hardly a good example."

"She's a perfect example of doing her own thing and being lauded for it. Now it's my turn."

"Good for you. Let's go in and have a nice cup of tea." He took my elbow guiding me in while giving James his psychologist's leave-her-to-me look, flashing an idiotic smile at me.

From the bathroom I heard whispering and shushing and a door banging as I washed the cochineal from my wrinkles. When I came out James had gone.

"Where's James?"

"Gone to buy food and wine and collect John from the airport. We're going to have a party." he said jovially.

He'd never make an actor.

"I emptied all the food into the bin before I left," I said.

He didn't know what to say but his eyes said she's flipped.

"I'm not going back, ever."

"You really shouldn't take Colette seriously, she's a very silly woman."

"Colette's a lot of things but she's not silly. I'm the silly one. Thick as bottled pig shite actually."

"Auntie Nora, I'm shocked. I never heard you say anything like that before."

"I thought it though, I've a mind like a sewer."

That shut him up. We drank our tea watching the clock loitering.

"Uncle Ben?" he ventured when the silence stretched too long.

"The same pompous ass."

Poor Andrew, his smug I'll-sort-her-out look completely faded. Skid marks lined his forehead as his thoughts raced looking for a slot to fit me into. Give him his due he didn't seem to be going straight into menopausal.

"I'm not so much running away as launching myself."

"Oh yes!" he said leaning forward in his earnest you-can-tell-me-anything position, ready to blind me with psychology, labels already gumming up, wickedness enters the new me.

"Andrew," I said, "do you ever hear voices?"

Eureka, his face bloomed. "Eem, well no, but . . . "

"Neither do I."

Murder flickered across his transparent face. I smiled my fuddy-duddy auntie smile.

"Would you like to lie down, John won't be here for hours."

"Yes," I said to his obvious relief.

I lay in Andrew's bed too tired and afraid to sleep. Eventually I drifted into a nightmare chased by Ben looking for food. I'm making custard, stirring and stirring, watching it curdle, brown flecks appear and grow and grow enveloping me. I jumped out of my dream smothering in the brown duvet, panicking.

I crept out. James was assembling herbs and things.

"Sleep well?"

"Yes thank you," I said lurching into the bathroom. My face even more rucked from fretful sleep.

James arrived bringing food and drink. And John.

John made a fuss saying he was surprised to see me but showing none. I am surprised. Amazed actually. Glad the punk had warned me. John looked like an ad for good clean living. All collared and tied and beautifully suited. Whisper, whisper went James into Andrew's ear, cheering Andrew up no end.

James cracked jokes. Andrew made dinner and John entertained us with his American escapades. Enthralled, I couldn't take my eyes off his blond hair. It looked so real.

"My last sermon was something else," he said. "Looking straight into the camera I said, 'Dominus illuminatio mea', paused for two seconds, then, 'Thy light is my light'. The studio lights sort of illuminated me and I said, 'Cast thy bread upon the water for thou shall find it after many days,' and the bread came rolling in." He guffawed. So did James and Andrew.

"You're incorrigible," Andrew said.

"They're rich and if they didn't give it to me they'd spend it on drugs and drink. I'm saving them from themselves. My agent said . . . "

"Agent?" I shrieked.

"Yes mother, Jesus had John the Baptist touting for

him and I have Brian. He's having T-shirts printed with
'The Gospel according to Jonathan' in Gothic lettering
across the front and back."

"Who's Jonathan?"

"Me, I'm starting my own church, more money in it
and he has a great idea for you . . ." his voice trailed off,
his face pinking.

"When you're more yourself," James jumped in.

"Who am I when I'm not myself?"

His eyes passed me over to John.

"You know, the way you were before, the mother we
knew and loved."

I stared him down. Andrew went straight for the
jugular and hacked the chicken to bits. I forgot to
breathe. Pain surged through me, converting me. I asked
my sons, "Is a meat cleaver the same as a bolt from
heaven?"

Neither answered but gave each other a jaded look.

"I mean, are all conversions instant?"

They were bemused.

"I've just had an instant conversion."

"Conversion to what?" James asked tightly.

"Vegetarianism. No light or voice, just the belt of a
meat cleaver and I turn into a vegetarian. My running
away was the same, instant. I didn't hear a voice
saying, 'Run Nora run'. I must be open to conversion at
the minute but who's converting me now that I'm an
atheist? Even that was instant. If I'd run away yesterday
when I was still a believer, would God have looked
after me? If I was naked would he have thrown a robe
to me?"

"More than likely the police would and probably charge you."

"Yes, I suppose. Anyway I haven't that sort of courage. As it is I change my clothes and you no longer know or love me. It must have been just cupboard love." I laughed and laughed. They didn't.

"Of course you're still our mother." John's wig moved sincerely.

James examined his nails and swooped on a hangnail and nibbled hungrily at it. Eyes down, Andrew chopped, sealing my conversion.

John said, "It's like this, mother . . . " then petered away, losing track.

"Come, come, John, you who preaches to millions and amazes them with your bilingual oratory, surely can articulate your feelings to your poor old Mum."

He couldn't or wouldn't. James's eyes slid from his fingers down the table.

"What it boils down to is I've no identity outside a dowdy skirt and an apron."

"No, no," my sons chorused while their cousin chopped.

Shock filtered through their protestations as I lit a cigarette, drew the smoke down inside me and savoured. Blowing out slowly.

"Another instant conversion," quipped John.

Sucking deep I said, "No, I've been smoking quite a while now. Took it up to shorten my sentence." I coughed gaily.

"But you have everything, beautiful home. State-of-the-art kitchen."

68

"Everything a good housewife needs but I've given up housekeeping."

"You can't." John said sternly.

"I can and I did. I'm finished with housework forever."

They were offended. I took a deep drag, screwed up my eyes and said, "Colette, what about Colette?"

"Surely you're not comparing yourself to Colette," James sniggered.

"Why not?" I dare them to specify.

"She's different," John said cautiously.

"You can bloody well say that again."

A communal wince at bloody. Andrew stopped chopping. The pan sizzzled perfuming the air with garlic. Chicken was added, with peppers and herbs. My stomach cramped. Sagging with hunger I lusted after the chicken. I tried to police my rampant desire but excuses popped up for postponing my vegetarianism. What was the harm? Made no difference. The chicken was already dead. Already cooked even. Couldn't refuse the proffered meal. Shame and seduction blend and battle. Battery hen, I said to myself fiercely but I still wanted to eat the chicken. I was despicable.

My sons examined me. Did they see the cracks, the shallowness, the drool about to spill? I outstared them.

"Andrew," I blurted out, "I won't be able to eat that delicious chicken."

"Aunt Nora! I am definitely losing my touch. I thought you'd yield to temptation or postpone your conversion with a touch of St Augustine's 'not yet' syndrome," he baited.

69

"Actually I was hoping you'd offer an alternative to scorched flesh."

I dealt the lie to him and watched. He knew. They all knew, could see I wanted the chicken.

"I'll make you an nice savoury omelette. My eleventh hour specialty and an *instant* side salad."

A titter slipped from John's lips.

"Thank you Andrew, but I'm quite happy to eat cake."

"No trouble and anyway we've no cake."

"No eggs thank you," I said, "I've just turned vegan. Bread will do and an instant salad."

He had the grace to blush.

Fortified I said, "Tell me, how is it that Colette can plough her erratic furrow while I'm coffined in the straight and narrow for ever."

"Colette is Colette," James said stupidly.

"You know I'd rather be bludgeoned to death in New York or mowed down in Mozambique than continue the lingering fossilisation mapped out for me."

"Dad, what about Dad?" accused John.

"What about him? I'd rather be a baglady than go back to him."

Their mouths pleated with disapproval.

I did not like the adults my children have become. I did not like John. I did not like James. Or Andrew for that matter. I did not like any of them. I felt light. Free. I waited for a bolt from heaven to blast me off the face of the earth. No blast. I waited suspended for the guilt to blot out my joy. Only guiltless relief. I was so happy. So

70

free. I wanted to love them again but I settled for loving all mankind.

"Me," I shouted. "What about Meee?"

Six eyes looked at me, bewildered.

"Me, John, what had your agent in mind for me?"

"Oh that, forget it."

"No, tell me please."

"It's irrelevant."

"Ah go on," I cajoled.

He sighed and in his flattest monotone said, "A good Christian mother in her thatched cottage in rural Ireland, cooking spuds over an open fire talking about her immovable faith. That's it."

"Why not have her barefoot as well?"

"With your feet!" they said in spontaneous union.

"Why not?" I laughed, "they'd add character. Zoom the cameras in on my poor bunioned feet resting on the hearth beside my hob-nailed boots."

"Yes, yes I like it," John said in spite of himself.

"How much?" I said.

"What!"

"How much would I get?"

"You mean you'd do it?"

"Why not, if the money's right."

Winks snaked between James and John.

"Don't forget the nudge nudge," I sniped.

Muttering half-hearted sorries, I glimpsed the two little boys they once were and my heart crimped remembering what little sleeveens they were even as children.

"You can haggle over fees during dinner," Andrew said setting the table.

And haggle we did and ate and laughed. The wine was good. I drank a lot and ate bread. Lolling about after dinner we reminisced. Their childhood when the sun always shone and Andrew was always with us.

The doorbell rang. I knew instantly. They looked at each other but not at me. Ben had come for me. I went with him. I didn't say a word. And haven't spoken since.

I've nothing to say, except . . . except . . . I wish I was Colette.

Football Crazy

*A*ll night long the ball bounces and bangs. The dry hard thud slams my skull and grinds my brain. I grit my teeth and harden my jaw against the onslaught. And the ball is locked inside my head.

I sit and wait in the surgery. Babies whinge and mothers gossip. One goes through her five pregnancies, pain by pain. Curly's mother is there, expecting another.

"One of each," she says cockily to mother-of-five.

"Young fella's football crazy," she hoots.

"Harmless fun," crones mother-of-five, cuffing her erring brat simultaneously.

Curly's mother stiffens. Her lips disappear.

"Not to some it isn't." She nods towards me.

I sink into the sticky plastic upholstery.

"Frustrated aul bitch can't let innocent children play just cos she's none of her own. Can't get a man so she takes it out on the kids," she stage-whispers, sniggering.

"Ah now, Miss Brophy, you're letting this little matter get on top of you, a bit of a persecution complex. After all they're only children."

His face is fair and pink. Eyelashes white. He paces

75

up and down. His neck creases into his collar and balloons into jowls. He tries to jolly me along.

"Let's not take this business too seriously, what?"

The ball is heading into the net of my brain.

His eyes swoop over my body. Tissue-paper flesh, ghosting bones.

"What age are you?"

"Thirty-eight."

That startles him. His jowls jelly. I almost laugh.

"Well now, we have been letting this little matter take its toll, haven't we?"

He's more used to mumps and measles and snotty-nosed kids.

"Have you approached the parents?"

"They abuse me."

"The local priest?"

"Don't know him."

"Other neighbours?"

"They don't want to bring them on themselves."

"Family?"

"Brother in Australia."

The healer is a quivering mass of helplessness. A smile lurches across his face.

"Take up a hobby." He tries to think of something.

"Eh, eh, meals on wheels."

He feels as ridiculous as he looks. He laughs at himself. "I mean when we fatten you up a bit."

"I could eat if you took away the ball."

"Yes, yes." He pulls his rubbery lips thinking furiously. His lips sling back into place. He smiles.

"How about a holiday?"

"It's too late. He'll come with me, knocking the food out of my mouth with the football."

"I see, I see."

He pokes his ear, looking for guidance.

"I'll give you some tranquillisers. They should help." He fumbles in his thick brown bag and produces a bottle. He scribbles on a label and sticks it on the bottle.

"Take one when you go home. And two going to bed and come back next week. No, Wednesday, come back this Wednesday. In the meantime I'll make an appointment for a friend of mine to see you."

Nervousness blinks his eyes and jerks his words. He lets me out. The thought of passing the buck relieves him somewhat. But the lines around his eyes knit worriedly.

They're there. Taking up their position on my wall. Their leers lick across the garden. Almost touching me.

One, two, three, four, five, six, seven, all good children . . . I wish them in hell. Curly spots me watching from behind the curtain. He gives me the two-fingered sign.

God, please send the rain and wash them off my wall.

"Right lads, let's get the show on the road."

"Ah lay off, Curly, she looks awful. She's all crumpled like an aul paper bag."

"She is an aul bag. Now kick it or else."

"OK, OK, but I'm not followin' it into her garden."

"Who asked ye, ye cretin, don't I always get it meself?"

He kicks the ball high in the air. The dry hard crack

tears my roses and enters my head. Thorns of roses embedded in my head. Tear clouds brew and clog my eyes. He waves.

I switch on the television loud, very loud. Ironically, it is feverishly hawking headache cures. It doesn't blot out the thwack of the ball. Nothing does. Even at work, the click of computers doesn't drown it. Anorexia nervosa whispers in the air. No one mentions diets anymore. I take three tranquillisers as the ball jerks my head back and forth, splitting my nerve ends. I lie on the couch wishing for a miracle. A miracle called John. If only he'd come again like he did last year. Out of the blue.

It was an exquisite day. Best all summer. High on the beauty of the day, I passed Curly's house. The gentle multi-coloured sweet peas delicately trailed the wall, delighting the eye and perfuming the air. Six standard roses stood unnaturally still. Three gaudy gnomes fished in a plastic pond in a perfectly manicured lawn. I wanted to dash in and rescue the sweet peas. As I turned the corner into my own street, Curly slid off my wall, grinning. Waiting for me to witness the destruction of my garden. The day wintered.

I lock myself into the tiny stuffy kitchen to escape. My spirit dropping into biliousness. I unpack my few groceries. A soft thud on the kitchen window shivers through me.

He can't be here. Not at the back of the house. I smother the sound in pretence. Hairs stand to attention on my arms. I stare vacantly into presses. Fat tins, full to the brim, stare back at me. Again a knock, decisive, impatient, traps me and the door handle moves. I close my ears but my eyes drag to the door and watch the handle snap. Throwing my eyes up to the window, a huge face grins at me. I solidify.

"Aren't you going to let your little brother in then?"

Brother hangs in icicles in my mind.

"It's me, Aileen, don't you recognise me?" His smile waning.

John, warm, safe, brother John slots into place, uprooting, unlocking, unchaining, throwing me into massive protective arms. Hugging mugs of coffee we exchange gossip. Mine two carrier bags full of deaths and who's gone away. His funny little anecdotes about down under. And then we slip joyously into the past. Into the garden where the hawthorn grew. Strawberried and apple blossomed as only childhood gardens can be.

The ball smashes into the magic garden and crashes against the hall door. John jumps up and watches Curly slowly, carelessly swagger up the path, pick the ball from the trembling flower bed and mash his heel into the ground. John jerks open the door. Curly turns smirking. In two strides John has him by the scruff of the neck. Curly drops the ball and John drops Curly outside the gate. His face a perfect question mark freckled with fear.

Ten minutes later, Curly's da bullies along on short legs. His backside twisting vigorously, trying to keep up with his indignation. Curly and the cronies follow. The little man hammers on the door.

John opens it wide, filling the space.

"Well?" His voice swells the street.

"I, I've come about the ball."

"What about it?"

"I was wonderin' could the lad have it back."

"I," booms John, "was expecting you to apologise for that gurrier."

"Now there's no need to be offensive," says the little man puffing up an inch with aggro.

"Give it to him, Da," shouts Curly, desperately eyeing his mates at the gate.

"Give me what?" bellows John.

Curly's pals begin to jeer.

"Da," accuses Curly, "ye said you'd get me ball back or burst him."

"What?" John's frame expands.

"Now mister, I didn't come here to fight," says the little man shrinking into his jacket. "A pity," John says rolling up his sleeves.

Curly's da tries again with all the bravado he can muster while fright ghosts his dentures.

"I'd appreciate it very much if you could see your way to giving it back."

"No."

The dentures snap or fall shut.

"I'll have the law on you," he says half-heartedly.

"Do that."

The little man starts to move off. The gang watch. He hesitates. He looks at John. He looks at Curly. He looks at the mocking crowd at the gate. He thinks of his wife. She'll kill him. He turns again to John.

"You know of course the lad is sorry, very sorry, I might add."

He pushes Curly forward.

"Tell the man you're sorry," he hisses, squeezing the boy's arm, hard.

Curly gets the message. "I'm sorry, mister."

"Are you sure, boy?"

"Yes sir, I'm sure," Curly whinges.

John sticks his broad tanned face into Curly's pale one.

"You had better be, boy, you had better be."

He planks the ball into Curly's chest, slightly winding him.

Father and son try to swagger out. Curly holds the ball high above his head.

"Look lads, didn't I tell yis me da'd get it back."

The gang move away silently.

The garden budded and bloomed and blossomed. Then John went away.

He had gone about a month when Mrs Brown sweeping nosily around the path collars me.

"Haven't seen that handsome brother of yours for ages. Where are you hiding him?"

She leans on her brush, her eyes hungry. Always when she's looking for information she uses the brush as a prop. My mouth opens without engaging my brain.

"He's back in Australia."

By the end of the week they all knew and Curly was back with a vengeance.

One, two, three, four, five, six, seven battered months. My head is a swollen bruise. The tablets are pressing my eyelids into sleep, trapping the ball inside. I try to keep one eye open but it falls shut.

A ribbon of terror circles my head and knots. Squeezing the ball off the wall of my skull in slow motion soundlessly, into my throat. I gulp in large quantities of air. Sucking like a greedy baby. But the ball gags. I dry retch. And run for the carving knife.

I awake. There is total peace. Ball gone. Head empty. Only sound, running water. Somewhere beautiful. The garden. The magic garden, strawberried and apple blossomed with a stream gurgling and splashing. But there was no stream in the garden where the hawthorn grew. My eyes open. Red hot liquid rushes past gurgling and gushing over my outstretched hand, down the polished parquet hall.

The ball slams the door, scattering and blobbing blood everywhere. It gathers again in a single stream and trickles under the hall door following the ball as it comes to rest in the roses. And gluts around it. Curly swaggers up the path leering as usual.

Humpty Dumpty

"This sandwich is not happening for me," he said. His legs like uncooked sausages dangling loose from his shorts.

"Excuse me?" the waitress said, a forced smile cracking through her lips. It came with the job.

"This sandwich isn't happening for me, it's eh uum, you know?"

"I'm afraid you've lost me, sir." The smile set aside.

Of all the eating joints in New York, this motherfucker has to choose this one. And of all the tables in the cafe he has to park at mine, Patricia Dockrell thought. Must be nerds' day out. Her fourth already and she had barely started her shift. Michele always got the exotic ones, like the dominatrix in her flowing robes with her young men on leads, salivating at her feet.

"I had a cutlet sandwich here before and it was amazing."

"In what way, sir?" she asked in an enamelled grind.

She'd have to stop doing that. Wrecking her teeth. The teeth her mother spent hundreds on while her own rotted.

"It had everything," he said.

85

She stone-eyed him. She knew if he hadn't pale sausage legs that would sizzle at the hint of a sunbeam, she wouldn't be giving him such a hard time but then again he was the fourth eejit of the day. A bad day.

A bad day at the end of a bad week.

All week long she'd been waiting for the phone to ring. William to call. Ask her to his party. He'd already asked Carol.

"That sandwich has everything, chicken breast, avocado, bacon, mayonnaise on foccaccia," she said on the cusp of a yawn.

"Yeah but it's lacking uuumph, you know!"

He was getting to her and she was losing her cool. She used to go out of her way to be kind to customers like him until they took to asking her out.

Hostility tugged at her right eye setting it fluttering, which at times had been interpreted as a wink. To the beholder's cost.

"Give me a break, I only stand and serve when my legs aren't going like egg beaters between table and kitchen," she said.

"Pardon me, I'm only a customer, a dissatisfied one at that."

"Which bit isn't up to scratch?" she snapped.

"The whole lot sucks."

She snatched the plate. "Excuse me *sir* while I tell the chef about his sandwich's poor performance. He will not be pleased. If you see a man coming at you with a machete, duck."

"Thank you for sharing that with me."

"What's up doc?" Michele said as they collide in the kitchen door.

"The nerd wants a sandwich with attitude."

"Tell him they're all laid back today," Michele said in a hail of giggles.

"I want to poison him. Run the guts out of him."

"No word then?"

"What?"

"William."

"He's asked Carol. She's borrowed my green skirt."

"That's our Carol. She'd borrow your knickers and give them back dirty."

Michele hates Carol. The one thing she borrowed from her was Harry and she never got him back, not even in rag order.

"I really thought you'd connected with William after the *Get Shorty* movie. The way he singled you out."

"Yeah. And the play."

She had gone to see him perform.

Afterwards at "The Scratcher", their local pub, she told him how great he was and he smiled and talked about great roles he intended playing. He walked her home. Kissed her lightly, said he'd call.

Days rollerbladed past in a sticky hot haze of yellow cabs, and still her mouth had an upward tilt. She had the hots for him. A real sweetie. If she called any bloke that, where she came from, she'd end up in intensive care. He reminded her of Henno. Beautiful Henno who laid down his life for her.

She rehearsed spontaneous replies. Light, witty but not too witty, not giggly, for when William called.

He didn't call on Monday. Or Tuesday. By Wednesday she began to panic. She kept testing the phone to see was it working. Should she ring him? He had given her his card. William Green, Actor.

She phoned him twice but, when she heard his deep seductive voice on the answering machine, she couldn't speak. Even though she'd had elocution lessons. Never dropped her aitches. Her mother had seen to that.

Thursday she found words. Left them on the answering machine. No reply.

Blew it, gobbing, she chided herself.

Friday she left a crisp upbeat message. No reply.

Today Saturday. Party time. No invitation. And she was taking it out on the customer with the white flabby legs.

"Maybe he lost your number or something," Michele said.

"Yeah."

Michele is her mate. Closer than the rest. But not too close. The only one to call her Doc. Has done since Sharon Brown appeared in the cafe a month previous.

"Jaaaasus, Doc," Sharon roared, flinging herself on Patricia.

"Patricia was the brain box of the school. We were all dead jealous. Went to college, got first class honours. The only one on the whole estate," Sharon told Michele, her words punctuated with flecks of food.

"See that," she said running her finger down her crooked nose. "She done it. Broke me nose when we were ten and I got me head done in for it. Never laid a finger on her and I got the grief."

Patricia laughed. "It's the thought that counts and you were going to give me a going over."

"Just a few digs but you gave me the head."

"Would I do such a thing, Michele?"

Michele looked from one to the other.

"I brought me Ma around to sort her out and what happens? I get beaten about the head all the way home."

Patricia remembered the day well.

All week long Sharon had been needling her. Mimicking her posh accent. Pushing and shoving, finally pinning her to the railings. Calling her a stuck-up bitch, teacher's pet and her mother a slut. Trapped by Sharon's sturdy body, Patricia head-butted her and ran home in fright, speckled in Sharon's blood. Told her mother all.

"You did the right thing," her mother said.

Although she called herself Missus, she defended Patricia with the fierceness of the single mother she was and still is.

"But you don't understand, she's one of the Browns."

Fright flickered in her mother's eye momentarily.

"Strategy is all," her mother said giving her a lollipop and the two of them climbed the stairs. They sat on the bed and waited.

Patricia wished her Dad was there to defend them. He was massive according to her mother. Bigger every time she described him and better. Scandinavian. Blond and beautiful. A Viking to see off the Browns.

Dusk fogged the street light across the road. The "graveyard" they called that spot. The place where all torched cars ended. They often watched car chases from that window. Stolen cars driven at high speed, screeching brakes.

Through the foggy light, Mrs Brown larded along in her buckled sneakers. Sharon pointing out their house.

"Only two of them, no big deal. Don't come down, I'll handle this," Patricia's mother said.

Patricia sat in the dark at the top of the stairs watching shadows crawling up the walls from the sad lone bulb in the hall. Her mother pulled the door open sharply as Mrs Brown was about to knock leaving her swooning forward. Jowls quivering. Sharon, whose nose was now a swollen mass caked in dried blood, stood behind her.

"You're very good to call, Mrs Brown but the doctor said Patricia's going to be all right. He gave her an anti-tetanus. Lucky, very lucky, those aul rusty spikes. Children don't realise." Tuts shivering off her tongue.

Mrs Brown was gobsmacked.

"X-rays tomorrow," Patricia's mother said in the void, diluting Mrs Brown's case further.

"What about my Sharon?" Mrs Brown eventually said, a hint of an apology creeping in.

Patricia's mother smiled a sad little smile at Sharon.

"Don't worry, Mrs Brown, I'm not going to call the guards, you have enough on your plate. I won't mention the attack at the school either. We don't want labels attached to a little girl. Bully is a dirty word."

Sharon whimpered.

"Don't fret, Sharon, I'm sure Patricia'll be all right. No GBH charge this time."

"But I didn't. I only . . . "

"Shut up Sharon and get home," Mrs Brown said swiping at her.

Sharon let out a wail.

"I'm sure she's learnt her lesson, don't punish her. The X-rays are only a precaution."

Mrs Brown pushed Sharon ahead of her down the path.

"Maybe Sharon would keep an eye on Patricia when she goes back to school?" her mother called after them.

"I'll see to it, Missus Dockrell," Sharon's mother said.

"Mind that little girl, me ma warned every bleedin' day," Sharon told Michele. "Me and me brothers, Patricia's minders. I wouldn't mind but she had the meanest karate chop. We used to set her on our enemies. They never suspected till it was too late."

Michele was cracking up.

"Everyone feels the need to look out for Patricia, shield her from the mean streets of Manhattan. Carol thinks she's silver spoon and all that. 'The Voice' she calls her. Thinks she's slumming in the East Village."

"Slumming! If you want to frighten the shite out of anyone you only have to mention our estate. Right Doc?"

"Right Sharon. An address to shudder at."

"I'm surprised you haven't head-butted that snotty cow, Doc," Sharon said.

"I will if the occasion arises."

"To think I felt I should mind you," Michele said.

"A culchie like you Doc's minder! Don't be wet."

91

"I'm not a culchie, I'm from Stab City," Michele said, immediately regretting calling her beloved Limerick that awful name.

"That's OK then. Next best thing to being a Dub."

Sharon didn't mention her brother. Henno. Nine months after the event. A different place and still unmentionable. Patricia felt disabled by the silence around his death.

Magnificent Henno. Dazzled by him. His dark wounded eyes that at once worried and wooed her. His earring twinkling. His dreadlocks. She was mad into him. Her mother kept warning her, giving her six packs of condoms.

"Henno's like your da. Hung like a stallion. Looks at you like a half starved beast."

"There you go again changing Da's image. From a Viking warrior, to a make-love-not-war marcher, to a half starved beast."

"He was all those. A gentle giant. Doesn't mean he hadn't the tackle and the passion."

"But Mam, I was a seventies' baby and that flower power thing was a sixties' phenomenon."

"The sixties didn't arrive in Ireland till the seventies," her Mother said, stepping over the truth.

Patricia reckoned her father was most likely a Nordic sailor.

"Henno'll jump you," she said.

He did.

"Don't get into a car with him," she said.

She did.

"He'll kill himself," she said.

He did.

"He'll kill you," she said.

He didn't.

He saved her.

"Robbing cars is better than shooting up," Henno said. "The buzz, deadly. The rush, better than Speed."

Henno stole cars for the pure joy of driving them. Never torched them. She went with him often. Was with him the last time.

The silver Jag. His favourite. Hot wiring. Coaxing. Purring. Cruising. His delicate twig-like fingers cupping the wheel. His bracelet clinking against the steering wheel. The moon a pale gold disk with a hairy Molly of a cloud tracking across its middle. The night wrapped around them. The sea swishing and retreating. Licking the tyres as they winged along the water's edge on the Bull Island.

A garda car eased up close. Henno's thumbs, like cocked hammers of a shotgun, pressed the wheel. Foot to floor. Chasing across the sands. Skimming the water. High speed merry-go-round. Blue dome-light revolving. Sirens whirring. Losing them. Then the lights of another coming at them. Pinning them in headlights. Blinding.

"Cover your face," Henno said blinking blindness away. Swerving, fishtailing. Streaking for the causeway. Braking, slamming into reverse, thumping and shuddering on to the creaking wooden bridge in a twirl of sand. Rocketing along. Speedometer jittering over ninety. The old bridge thrumming under them.

Police on their tail again as they headed for the main

road. Taking the roundabout the wrong way. Tossing, swaying, slicing up the road. Into the estate. Safe.

"Leg it as soon as I stop," Henno said. Eyes off road for a nanosecond.

The lamppost coming at her. Tangled in her scream. Henno jerking the wheel. Pumping the brakes. Burning rubber. Cartwheeling. Down to earth against the concrete. Tearing them apart while the current between them was still connected. Henno jarred and broken, bracelet clinking at the wheel. Dark blood worming from his nostril, sprouting pink from elsewhere. His ghost hissing away in a stream of blood while her nerve ends waved in static.

Faces upside down. Doc Martened feet in Henno's blood. Lifting. Separating. Click-clunk. Spiriting her away. The turn of the wheel condemning her to stay while catapulting Henno into infinity.

Henno was everywhere in his absence. In her dreams she tried to put him together again. But he kept falling apart. Pieces missing like a broken jigsaw. His hands were there. On the wheel, bracelet clinking. His face missing.

Her mother whispering grief. Patricia wanted to crawl onto Mrs Brown's ample lap, lie against her sagging breasts and talk Henno. Healing in the gilded words of his mother as she told her everything about him from his first tooth.

But all the Browns kept away in a shush of silence. A hushed up silence. A silent eraser. Rubbing her out of the picture. Out of the scene. Out of Henno's death.

The police rounded up the usual suspects excluding

the respectable Patricia Dockrell who had graduated from Trinity College the day of the crash.

Later, a long time later, Patricia saw the newspaper cuttings. The Jaguar, a pile of scrunched up metal. Henno smiling up from his Confirmation photo. Henno in black and white. Henno in technicolour. Now Henno in sepia. Henno's features dissipating, running together in a blur. Henno in the past tense. William in technicolour.

"What are you going to do about him?" Michele said.

"I won't go when he rings, say I'm otherwise engaged."

"Not William, I was talking about the jerk."

"Oh him, add some fresh lettuce and wish him a nice day."

"Have a nice day, sir," she said as the plate, in a spin, shuddered and shook on the table.

He smiled and asked her out.

Nine o'clock. Still waiting for William to phone full of remorse at not returning her calls and begging her to come to his party.

She tested the phone. Perfect tone.

"Asshole," she told her mirror image at half past nine as she squeezed two small zits that had sprouted on her forehead. "Read my lips, William used you to get Carol, who is only interested in other girls' blokes. He is not going to ring. Period."

She tested the phone again. Her lips dragged down, acknowledging.

"Wouldya look at William pouting at himself in the

mirror. Make you puke," Michele said as they sat at the bar in their new gear.

William and his little gang in a huddle, posing. Artificial laughter tingling. He saw them. Whispered to Carol as he patted her bottom. Finger printing Patricia's green skirt.

"Bastard," Michele said.

"Yeah. I was a right eejit fancying that shithead," Patricia said.

"Yeah. Oh, oh, here comes Carol. Maybe we're getting a late invitation."

"Listen you guys, you are not invited and I wouldn't advise gate-crashing."

"I beg your pardon," Patricia said in her snootiest flutiest voice. Her neck elongating like an indignant swan. "We've no intention . . . "

"In that gear! don't give me that crap."

Patricia stuck her face into Carol's.

"Now listen here, slag, I may be dressed to kill but I've no intention of doing so. On the other hand with a nod of the head I can smash your expensive rhino job to smithereens," Patricia said barely above a whisper.

Carol's hand flew to her nose.

"Now piss off and tell slimeball Willie we don't want to go to his poxy party."

Carol nodded and scurried back to William, her face putty, clammy, eyes out of their lids.

"She was dead lucky," Michele said.

"Dead safe, I never damage a messenger, not physically anyway."

"Just frighten the shite out of them, as Sharon poetically put it," Michele laughed.

William, using his smile, sidled over. Hand on Patricia's shoulder.

"It's William the turd," Michele said.

"Carol was out of order. Jealous cow," he said lashing his charm. "Please come to my party, girls," his head tilting in a plea.

"No thanks," Patricia said.

"Better go out into the highways and byways, I'm sure you'll find someone desperate enough," Michele said.

"And another thing, Willie . . . " Patricia said.

"William please, I'd prefer if you called me William," he said. His face closing in a wince.

"Do me a little favour, William," Patricia said seductively.

"Sure."

"Go easy mauling Carol's ass when you two are fused in sweat. I don't want greasy paw marks on my skirt when she gives it back."

He stood. Gaping.

"Run along, Willie." The iced words clink.

"Bitch," he hissed and stomped off.

They watch him go, slyly rubbing his palms on his trousers.

"You got him. Straight to his Achilles' heel. I didn't know he had sweaty hands."

"He hadn't, but he has now and will have forever."

"That's what I call long term revenge," Michele yelped.

Patricia's eyes filled up. Huge watery tears plopped.

"Don't let that prick get to you."

"It's not him . . . Not that flashy creep." Patricia

hiccoughed leaving the bar in a drizzle of tears, Michele at her heels.

"I'm going home to put Henno together again, piece by piece," Patricia said as they walked in the soupy hot air of the East Village.

"Who's Henno?" Michele asked.

"One of the Browns."

A Piece of Cake

*T*he cold hard sun shone through him. The beginning of a new year. He himself began at the end of the year. November, murky November. Seventy-eight or was it nine on the fifteenth?

A shaky sigh fizzled out of him. Mr Johnson prided himself on not being deceived by the camouflage of budding beauty and stretching days. He knew the east wind was hiding behind the crocused purple, orange and white skirts of flowery newness. Gnarling, sneakily ready to rip open chilblained wounds.

Winter always bullied into February. Refusing to call back biting winds. It took Chrissy last year. He wouldn't put his nose outside the door till real spring. This decision, and his own cunning, pleased him. He made tea. Carefully scalding the pot. Lid and all. Just like Chrissy used to do. Daughter Ann did it too. Not like young Christine. Christine threw a tea bag into a cup, swirling it around, mashing it against the side of the mug then dragging it out by the scruff of the neck, like a drowned rat.

Christine was on his mind. At the back, worrying and upsetting him. Sometimes Christine made the blood rush around his body in angry gallops. Even made his

101

dead feet hum with effrontery. Yet he couldn't pinpoint this aggravation.

Did Ann tell him? She was always feeding him bits and bobs of information. Couldn't grasp who she was talking about half the time. Ruination skidded into his thoughts and linked with Christine. Whatever ruined Christine floated out of reach. But he clung like a burr to Christine and ruin. He sipped his tea sitting at the fire. Poking and prodding till it lost its glow. He shivered at the loss of heat.

Women's something floated into his head. Women's what?

Women detached from his brain and he was left bewildered. Chrissy would have remembered. Sharp as frost, remembered everything. Sucked up information like a sponge and stored it. Then squeezed out every minute detail till his head was swollen with carrier bags of useless information. Mostly about the neighbours. He had learnt to switch off. But never learnt to switch on fully again.

His head was like a turned-down hearing aid with midges of words swimming around out of reach. Even Chrissy wasn't clear anymore. She had taken over Ann's body. Voice and all.

He tried to isolate her in old age. But it was no use. He could only see her in Ann's middle-aged body or young and nubile when he was chasing her. He was a great man for the ladies. Casanova Johnson. Mothers used to warn their daughters about him. He tried to conjure up the sinful excitement of it all but couldn't even register a bad thought. He dozed, mouth hanging slack, drooling pools into his cardigan.

He travelled down the dank school corridors into a rough brown desk. His heart beating in frenzy as the winged nun's shadow fell on him. The word of God, so lovingly taught on his mother's comfy lap, emptying out in fright. The nun beating the Catechism into his swollen chilblained hands. She left him throbbing to pick on another. Not the doctor's curly-headed daughter or the solicitor's sly son. No, Sister Declan, thin and bitter as a lemon, descended on poor little Phyllis Potter. Stick twitching at the ready. Vulnerable little girl who looked like a boy in a dress. Her head, barely pricked with hair, rose neckless above a ragged jumper. Thick buttonholes, awkward without buttons, stood gaping on her thin shoulder. Elbows red and raw poked shyly out of the ravelling mess. A wafer-thin summer dress hung desolately out of season from beneath the jumper. Her purple-grey spindly legs sprouted out of coarse, oversized black boots, tied with string. Solitude hung around her. And she never uttered a word. Her meek eyes bemused as the holy nun beat her with demonic fury. And the old man shouted in his dream "Stop, leave her alone." And the nun turned and her shadow fell on him. He awoke fending off blows. And cried for little Phyllis Potter.

"Suffer little children," burst from his lips in sadness and rage.

Anger set his brain wheeling. He became excited. Words fell thick and fast like snowflakes. He snatched at them. Heart racing as they jig-sawed into place. He knew what he wanted to say to Christine. He rehearsed it over and over. Careful not to let a word slip away. Then the doorbell rang. Scattering the daisy-chain of words. Spilling all over his head. He tried to gather them but they settled singularly in the arid wasteland. The bell rang louder, longer, clearing his head. Altogether.

He slippered to the door.

Christine and what's-his-name and the soft pink baby crowded the porch. He stood on the doorstep while the love of the baby oozed and trickled through him. They sort of bunched forward. Hinting to let them in. He stepped back slightly. They rubbed past him, Christine protecting a tea-towelled plate. What's-his-name, the baby? The baby grabbed the old man's face wobbling his glasses down his nose. Love caught in the old man's throat.

"Come in, come in," he said when they were already in.

What's-his-name plonked down, whistling the cushion. Delighting the baby. Christine, twirling magician-like, whipped the tea-towel from the plate with a "voila", revealing a chocolate fudge cake. His favourite.

"Baked it myself." She blushed.

A globule of tear swam in the old man's eye and spilt. Chrissy would have been pleased. He was pleased. What's-his-name was pleased. Everyone was pleased.

Something in the back of his mind was not pleased. His hands, tying in angry knots, knew what was wrong but didn't tell. What's-his-name probably knew but wouldn't tell. Anger rushed from his hands and aimed at what's-his-name. Who didn't notice. They were all loose and happy.

"Tea in the pot," said Mr Johnson.

"How long?" smiled Christine.

"Long, long, what has long to do with anything?"

"How long is it since you made the tea?"

Time tick tocked monotonously around his head.

He shrugged.

Christine patted his arm. "I'll make fresh stuff."

The baby jigged up and down on what's-his-name's knee. Up and down. Baby, happy baby. A warning light flickered in his head. Christine brought in tea and slices of chocolate fudge cake. He bit deep into the chocolate fudge and tasted childhood. Just like his mother used to make. And wife and daughter and now granddaughter. She had at last seen the light. Light panicked him. A warning light switched on, baby joined in, danger, baby. Danger for the baby, Christine not doing the right thing.

Christine said gaily, "I'm starting in the big bad world tomorrow. Imagine me an executive. No more mind-boggling decisions about which powder washes whitest." She laughed, peacocking around.

Mr Johnson's head thumped. His heart lurched. The danger lights blazed. Words strung together and splattered out with the chocolate fudge cake.

"Shouldn't go to work and leave the baby. Woman's place in the home. Man the breadwinner. Women's lib, feminists, all wrong. You shouldn't let her do it, Paul." (What's-his-name became Paul and in his anger Mr Johnson didn't notice.) "You can't go," he shouted. "I won't let you go and leave the baby with childminders."

The word childminder frilled with terror attached to orphanages, orphanages attached to nuns, nuns to Sister Declan and his heart squeezed with pain. The soft pink baby in the hands of . . . The pain locked and bolted inside him. Christine was talking to him. Her qualifications, her addiction to numbers, how she loved her little sums. His face shuttered. She held his bunched hand.

Paul came over and put the twittering baby on the old man's lap. The baby's podgy hand pulled at the old man's face, gurgling. Tears swam in the thaw and oozed out of his eyes. Spilling on the laughing baby. Christine cried. Paul gave her a let-me-handle-this look. He battled against the flow of the old man's tears, explaining gently, "No childminder, Grandpa, no childminder. We wouldn't leave the baby with a stranger. Ann, your daughter Ann, is going to mind the baby. And wait for it Grandpa, here is the best news, she's going to bring him to see you every day."

See the baby every day. Every day. The words knitted into a cosy pattern. Every day. He chuckled, hugging the baby. And began to tingle with the anticipation of it all.

Christine was doing the right thing.

The Ice Maiden

❖

*T*he boy stood at the counter. Meek. Isolated. New York fodder. The pain in the centre of his stomach had shifted and become a stitch in his right side. With every earnest nod, the new stiff collar of his shirt scraped the yellow-topped pimple on his neck.

His mother watched. Her body warped, straining forward at the ready. She had gone to the counter with him. And was banished by the cold American voice. A voice which addressed the nineteen-year-old as "sir".

"Who is this person, sir?" the interrogator asked.

A red flush enveloped the boy.

"Me mudder."

"Take a seat laydee, over there." The ice maiden pointed.

His mother didn't move. Her mouth opened. The boy wheeled around and stared at her. Loathing puked in his throat. He wanted to punch her "know-all" face. Stop the words coming out. The mother backed off wordlessly. Her top lip dropped, quivering, onto the bottom one and lapped.

Relieved, the boy almost smiled at her. Moving away grudgingly, she sat on the seat where the ice maiden pointed. Her fat carcass swelled over the edges. A strong

109

clip restrained her red and grey hair. But her freckled hands rolled around each other, demented.

Five had been interviewed since they had arrived. Alan and his mother heard everything. Everybody heard everything. Absolutely everything as questions and answers on earnings, savings, family, batted back and forth over the counter in the glass wall.

Faces of the refused tried to reassemble as the ice maiden's voice cut shards into them. Some lost the battle and disintegrated into mewling cries. One raw country lad she accused of having the look of a terrorist on their list and what's more, she said, would have to be investigated. Colour drained unevenly from his face, mottling it like a patchwork quilt, as he protested his innocence.

"Next," was all she said.

Alan's mother watched, hen-like. Surely some would have to get visas. Maybe even Alan. It could hardly be a totally negative day. Could it?

But the rejected all seemed more eligible, definitely more confident. Alan looked like a driven thing.

Questions hurled through the air at him, your purpose for going, who, where, what, when, how much?

The boy's answers fell stumbling and stuttering in a pile-up. The mother's face tightened. She wanted to ward off the hard flat questions flung into his callow face. Answer for him. He half turned to her. Her bottom left the seat. She bent forward. Lips activated. Poised to prompt. The voice pulled him back. His head swivelled, but his body stayed in the semi-curve. The mother perpendicular, lips moving silently, eased back to the

110

edge of the seat. And sat. Her leg began to hop. She kneaded it absently.

He hadn't a hope. An echo for that mouthpiece Declan O'Shea. Every single utterance was first chewed and regurgitated by that, that pervert. Terrible influence, pink hair at one time, half shaved another. And now if you don't mind, plaits. Like a girl. Once or twice she was on the verge of pointing this out to Alan but thought she might put ideas in his head.

When the friendship had started two years previously she was determined to put a stop to it. Had even gone to the school.

The priest, sucking a sweet, listened as she listed her grievances. A good boy, turned, changed utterly, answering her back, cheeking her, using language, voicing his opinion or more to the point, Decco's opinion.

"Do something," she ordered.

"Do something," the priest mimicked. "And what pray, had you in mind?"

"Separate them so that Alan can pal with someone else, more his own type."

"And what type is that?" the priest asked as the sweet slid in and out of his teeth.

"Well, you know, respectable and . . . " Her voice trailed off.

"More like himself?" the priest coaxed.

"Precisely."

"Introverted, shy, nervous, frightened, like Alan?"

He was blaming her. Pointing the finger. All her fault.

111

She attacked. "Alan was quiet, a good boy, a nice boy before . . ."

"Lonely, sad, a lonely sad vulnerable boy," the priest interrupted. "I asked Declan to take Alan under his wing. He did more, much more, drew him into his circle and became his friend. Alan's very lucky to have Declan looking out for him."

Blood galloped around her head in a frenzy.

"You can sit there sucking sweets and tell me not only do you approve of this friendship but actually foisted that, that weirdo on my Alan to lead him astray. I know what's best for my Alan, I'm his mother."

"If I were you, madam, I'd get down on my knees thanking God for Declan O'Shea. Alan's come on in leaps and bounds since they became friends."

"That's a matter of opinion. I thought you of all people would disapprove of his ilk. It would answer you better to expel that Decco rather than have him corrupt an innocent."

The priest stopped sucking. " I am not in the business of turning out an assembly line of lookalike, dressalike boys. All marching to the same tune. As an experienced psychologist, I'm concerned with the individual. Especially those on the margins. I sincerely hope Alan's small success isn't impeded. It would have grave consequences."

She left, hating the sweet-sucking priest even more than Decco. But she didn't stop the friendship. Oh no, no one was going to blame her, especially that pompous priest and his hard-boiled sweets. He hadn't even the decency to offer her one. Psychologist how are ya!

The hard American voice. The polite, menacing "sir". The mumbled replies. Hadn't she told him all the way to Dublin, all forty-seven and a half miles, to speak distinctly. He didn't say a word till she stopped the car. Then he turned on her. Accusing her, blaming her for his cramp, her greaseball of a breakfast solidifying in his stomach. Stuffing him into a shit suit, his hair hacked off like a bogman and the bloody shirt crucifying him, he said, dragging his tie and opening his top button. "No one dresses like this, jeans and casuals, even Docs, Decco said."

His mother convulsed. "That yobbo with a ring through his nose and his girly plaits, he's the reason, the sole reason I'm letting you go to Bridie."

Looking at her puce face and spittled mouth he backed off. He was terrified she'd hear around the town that Decco had already got his visa.

He buttoned his shirt, tightened his tie and got out of the car, gently closing it behind him. She sat gloating. Then followed.

Decco, yawning wide and careless, said, "Act cool. Charm the ice maiden, make her nipples stand out. Make her laugh." Decco swore he did. Claimed she was even on the verge of acceptance when he asked her out. "Dying for it," he said.

"Does your aul wan know I'm goin'?"

"No, I didn't . . ."

"No sweat, I know how she feels about me," he said flicking his hair. Confidence rippling through every plait.

"Says I've to stay with me auntie Bridie in Queens."

"Hickville," Decco said blowing smoke from his tiny fag.

"When she was over for Paddy's day she . . . "

"Jeeesus, not the one dressed in green with 'thank God I'm Irish' plastered across her chest?"

"That's me aunt Bridie." Alan laughed nervily.

"Gross, even worse than your aul wan."

"Yeah but the good news is, she's loaded. Mam says if I play me cards right . . . "

"You'll be in mortal danger from that rich bitch. Dangle the inheritance, make you a hostage of greed. Thirty years down the road, you'll be still at her beck and call and she'll probably leave it to the church. anyway."

"Hold it Decco. I'm only stayin' a few days, then leggin' it, say I've a job offer."

"You will, my son, have plenty of job offers. I'll fix you up as soon as we kiss the ground in Kennedy airport. Loadsa connections. And we'll live in Manhattan, on the Lowa-East-side," Decco said.

Last year Decco had spent the summer in New York living in the East Village just up from the "Hell's Angels" headquarters. Took part in the protest marches when the City closed the park to the down-and-outs. Had brilliant T-shirts depicting people with their heads smashed in and slogans saying, "I survived the Tompkins Park riots".

And Decco had the only Rastafarian hairdo in the town. Alan planned to ape him as soon as he hit the Big Apple. He'd have to add extensions to his mother-knows-best hair cut. Decco's mother was real cool, said nothing and the music cracking the walls. She braided Decco's hair, interweaving red and yellow silk thread through the plaits. Massive. She thought Decco was wonderful. Loved his gear. Even when he painted his Docs purple and green, called it artistic. No kiddin'.

The cramp in his stomach was reaching a crescendo. Sweat bubbling on his acned forehead. The ice maiden's jaw was clicking up and down, clipping the ends off words. He couldn't imagine anyone, even Decco, making her laugh. His eyes slid to her breasts. And immediately boomeranged back to her face.

She had stopped talking, waiting for an answer. The pain in his stomach rolled. He squeezed his cheeks together begging God, bargaining, promising Mass, even confession . . . Anything, anything but please God stop the greasy fry in his gut from errupting and whooshing down his leg like molten lava.

Like when he was ten. Running, running up the hill. the jamjar discarded. Implosion as he reached the kitchen and whoosh. His mother slapping him. Scalding his skinny legs. Shit everywhere.

Glad now Decco wasn't with him. He could just hear tell it . . . "Jeeesus, Mooney shat himself when the ice maiden spoke, leaving a yellow trail to the jacks."

He squeezed his buttocks numb, answering as the pain subsided. Barely holding on. Again re-entering negotiations with God. The ice maiden was handing him his papers. She almost smiled as she said, "Have a nice day."

Alan turned. His face splitting in a grin he gave his mother the thumbs up sign.

Her heavy jowl lifted. Lips unpleated. Smiling, she watched his narrow back and the flecks of blood on his new white collar as he ran. A tear rolled down her cheek and splashed on her large freckled hand.

Medusa Who?

❖

"**F**ilth," Aine's mother shouts down the phone as Aine sits at her desk in the community centre of a sprawling Dublin westside estate. "No other word for it. Have you seen the papers? Those dreadful pictures everywhere. Even the *Times*. Front page. In technicolour no less. I'm surprised at the government sponsoring such an exhibition."

"But Mum, ninety-nine per cent of the exhibits are noncontroversial." Aine says.

"Yes but who got the coverage, the filth. Massive coverage. One hundred per cent coverage of those evil paintings."

"They're not evil, they're depicting the evil men do to women."

"In the worst possible taste. Disgusting turds and penises. That art teacher has a lot to answer for."

"Debbie didn't . . . "

"I told you, didn't I, they'd be the ones the press would pick out."

"You did. But the paintings were inspired by the government's ad – It's a crime to beat a woman – "

"It's a long way from a voice on the radio saying 'It's a crime to beat a woman', to those crude pictures.

119

Taxpayers' hard-earned money being used on that vulgarity. I can see questions being asked in the Dáil about this."

The door opens. An enormous grin, gusting into a fullblown laugh, flows ahead of Debbie into the room.

"Have to go, Mum," Aine lies.

"You'll be sacked. Your first proper job at twenty-six and you've blown it."

"Bye Mum," sighing.

"Shock, horror?" Debbie giggles.

"And the rest. A lot of people were shocked."

"So they should be. They are shocking."

"Not shocked at the message, shocked at the paintings, some only saw dirty pictures."

"Oh well, like the poor, the morally outraged are always with us."

"I know. I was accosted by one who hissed I should remember my immortal soul and stop corrupting the good women of Ireland."

"A young bloke cornered me saying it was a manhating exhibition. It's art with a capital A and a clear message, I said. 'Cheap propaganda,' he said. Real men don't beat women and have nothing to fear from it, I said. 'It's an incitement to hatred of men, full stop,' he said. You're entitled to your perverse view, as all wife beaters are, I said."

"You didn't."

"I did and he said he'd be dug out of me. I rest my case, I said."

"You were lucky."

"I'm not afraid of anyone. Or anything."

"Hah, bet your big strong husband was less than a scream away."

"Just slightly more than a whimper. His shadow fell on your man and he legged it."

"I bet he did."

"This is brilliant publicity for our programme."

"Yeah, but I'm a bit worried about Josie. Sudden whoosh of fame like that just as she is emerging. Dangerous. I don't know whether I could handle it myself, even with my training."

"Lighten up, counsellor, you're a very negative person. It's everyone's dream to be discovered like that."

"But it all happened so quickly."

"Josie has guts, otherwise she'd never have painted the pictures in the first place."

"I suppose . . . You were very hard on Murph last night."

"No regrets. He deserved it."

"He's not the worst."

"Hold it right there Aine, I'm not going into that again."

"I'm only saying . . . "

"On your bike."

"What?"

"I said on your bike, I know you're only dying to see Josie."

"Well, I would like . . . "

"Then hop it, I'll hold the fort here."

"If you're sure?"

"I am."

"I can't believe it's only a fortnight since I found Josie curled up outside the centre almost frozen to death."

"Remember that when you see Murph. Give Josie my regards and tell her to dump that bastard."

"I'll give her your regards," Aine says lassoing herself with her scarf and clamping on her crash helmet. "See ya."

With her hands tight on the handlebars Aine recalled finding Josie.

Curled in an arc, Josie huddles in the doorway of the community centre in the weak morning sun. Bits of blue paint sprinkle her hair. One blue hand caressing the other.

"You're looking very blue," Aine says trying to sound light as she unlocks the door.

"Paint and cold. I'm perished. I'm here hours." Josie says moving forward like a warped plank, wrestling a heavy board before her.

"What's that?"

"Don't touch it, it's me painting, still wet."

Aine leans forward and sees only flecks of blue paint.

"The other side, ye eejit."

Aine puts her hand out to turn it over.

"Leave it, you'll only stick to it," Josie says. All emotion sucked out of her voice.

"Mind if I have a fag?" Josie says as she warms her hands on the hot mug of tea. Her narrow back still hooped from the cold.

"Feel free."

"I showed Murph my drawings, the ones Debbie said were great. 'Waste of good paper', he said, snithering and sneering. Then tore them up and trun them on the floor

122

mashing them with his heel. 'A waste of good paper' he said. I could feel me inside turning black, like a light went out inside me. Dead, you know like?"

Aine nods.

"And he put his fist into me face. 'That's it, finito. No more of that crap. You're not going up to that shower again, filling your head with nonsense, right?' I didn't answer him. He shouted. Gave me a few digs. I didn't feel anything, like it was happening to someone else. He went to bed. I heard him snoring. He tore up my drawings, smashed my spirit and he was snoring. He didn't want me to be anything only his toe-rag. That's all I'm ever going to be to him. Something to look down on."

"Oh Josie," Aine says, her eyes leaking tears.

"I thought he'd be proud of me. See I'm not useless. This time he'll be really proud, like when we were going out together. He used to call me his little canary. I was mad into him. A real bit of all right. Dead smart in his army uniform. Blowing his saxophone. Couldn't keep me eyes off him. My spic and span man." Josie shudders. "I tried to smooth the paper out, fit the pieces together like a jigsaw but it was no use. Then I took out the box of paints Debbie gave me and that piece of hardboard. I painted and painted. I painted my life, Aine. I painted my life with him. I used everything including a pot of blue paint from the shed. All night long I worked like a lunatic. Never felt tired or anything. On the other side of that board, Aine, is my life."

"May I?"

"Just be careful, your clothes could be destroyed."

123

Black and blue angst flood the painting. A half closed eye weeps down the board, swollen lips part revealing broken teeth. A bulbous nose pumps black-red into a pit of keys and curls. A yellow streak zigzags crazily across the blues and blacks.

"This is amazing . . . amazing. Wait till Debbie sees it."

"Gruesome, powerful, brilliant," Debbie says piercing the air with her squeals of excitement. Hugging Josie.

"This will be the centrepiece of our exhibition. You're a genius, a genius. I've discovered a genius. Oh Josie, next best thing to being a genius is discovering one . . . "

Debbie races out and drives off fast. Comes back with three bottles of champagne and glasses. Before Aine could ask, Debbie said she bullied a publican into giving them. Said she'd credit him as a sponsor in the brochure.

"To Josephine, a true artist," Debbie says raising her glass.

Josie is mortified. She and the rest of the women drink shyly. After a second glass Nan Doyle becomes garrulous. "I'm seventy-two and feel nineteen and wouldn't mind a toy boy." She hoots.

A lovely happy atmosphere descends on the place and they work with jokes hopping around the room. Nan, Peg, Sheila and Bernie are making a patchwork quilt, Theresa is making glove puppets, Josie painting and Dolores embroidering, Colette practising her calligraphy. Mary's pots lie drunkenly around her. They start with such possibilities but fall by the wayside as she nervily moulds.

Nan Doyle sings "The Auld Triangle" and the rest join in.

"What?" Aine asks as she feels Debbie staring at her.

"Did anyone every tell you you look like Orphan Annie with your Docs and shaved head?"

"All the time. My mother, every single time she sees me."

"I can just hear you singing 'Tomorrow, tomorrow'."

"My favourite tense is the present. Now, suits me fine. I feel fulfilled, privileged to be a facilitator here."

"They really took to you. Old Nan wanting to mother you when you said you were illegitimate. The sun shining on your little corn-stubble head and your skinny little legs sticking out of those heavy boots, as you told them you never knew your dad. A real tear jerker. I almost puked."

"It's true. I didn't, still don't."

"You forgot to tell them that when you were five, your mother married."

"I did tell them."

"A man of means and you became a poor little rich girl?"

"I didn't see the need to go into details."

"Just as well your mother sulked off last night before they copped on who she was in her drop-dead designer gear."

"I would have introduced her if she'd stayed. I've no hang-ups."

"Oh yeah! if . . ." Debbie tails off, distracted, squinting past Aine out the window.

125

"Would you look at that?"

"What?"

"Coming across the tarmac."

Aine sees a medallion man, spongey belly swinging low over tight jeans. He takes out a comb and runs it through his hair. A huge bunch of keys hangs from his belt slightly impeding his swagger.

"Grecian 2000. Permed. What could he want," Debbie sniggers.

"If he is, who I think he is," Aine says, "he's coming here to bury us not praise us."

"Jeesus, Murph?"

"The very man. Remember your Aikido lessons."

"John and Paul are up the corridor if we need them."

"We're supposed to be able to take care of ourselves."

"We are. It's a bonus to know two just men are only a scream away."

"I'd prefer twelve."

Murph kicks the door open with his cowboy boot, silencing the room. Sucks his stomach up to his chest. Slits his eyes in a Clint Eastwood mean look.

"You," he roars, pointing at Josie. "Get home."

Josie flicks a cold eye over him and continues to work.

"Howya Murph," Nan shouts, champagne high.

Faltering slightly, he gives her a belligerent nod as he pushes his way towards Josie. Debbie moves silently with speed and is before him, holding out her hand.

"Mr Murphy I presume, husband of my star pupil."

"Ye know bloody well who I am," knocking her hand away, "and I'm taking me wife out of this bloody kip."

"Only if she wants to go," Debbie says.

"She'll do what I tell her if she knows what's good for her."

He grabs Josie's arm. She jerks it back savagely.

"And you think you know what's best for this unique woman?"

"Unique me arse. She's a skivvy, nothing more nothing less and always will be no matter what notions you fill her stupid head with."

"She has the talent, I don't give her anything but encouragement."

"Don't give me that. You are deliberately coming between husband and wife."

"On the contrary, we aim to include husbands and families. Would you like to help us set up the exhibition? We could do with some strong men."

"Ah, I get it, you want free labour for teaching our women to get above themselves."

"Most of the husbands have already volunteered."

"More fools them." Turning to Josie. "Now are ye coming or do I have to drag ye."

"You're not dragging anyone from here, dickhead," Debbie says.

His face darkens into a suffusion of maroon and purple.

"Who are ye calling a dickhead?"

Debbie, Debbie, stop before it's too late. Can't you see he's bunching his hands, Aine screams inwardly.

"You, you nasty jealous prick," Debbie says.

"Oh that's lovely, that is. Foul language as well as

corrupting innocent women, getting them to draw men's private parts. What else is going on here I'd like to know?"

"That's David, Michelangelo's David."

"I know it's Michelangelo's bleedin' David. Do you think I'm ignorant?"

"Would you like to do a course yourself, Mr Murphy?" Aine jumps in.

He turns slowly and glares at her.

"Are you winding me up?"

"No of course not, John and Paul will . . . "

"John, Paul, George or Ringo won't anything. I'm not interested, full stop. Right?"

He turns to Josie. "Get up ye trollop and come on."

Josie doesn't move.

Coming up to screaming time, Aine decides, looking hard at Debbie who is either not tuned in or deliberately ignoring the warning signs. Read my mind, for God's sake, Debbie.

"Go home, Murph," Josie says coldly, not raising her eyes.

He sticks his face into hers. "I'm warning you . . . "

"You've no right to threaten her," Debbie says.

"Sez who?"

"Me."

"Oh yeah, well for your information, she's my wife and I'll do what I like. She'll pay for this and you will too. I'm going to inform the government about this den of iniquity, destroying marriages, teaching pornography and using disgusting language."

Debbie bursts out laughing. A nervous titter tinkles through the class.

"Bunch of bleedin lezzers that's all yis are."

"Go home and stop making an eejit of yourself," Josie says, drilling holes into him with laser eyes.

Murph hesitates. Hitches his jeans. And moves towards the door. "Wait'll I get you home, you'll get it," he snarls.

"You and whose army?" Nan shouts after him. But the rest cower.

Murph pauses. Ripples of fear shiver through the class. He goes, leaving the door ajar. Menace hangs in the air. Unfinished business.

What have we done? Aine asks herself. Josie could be killed and it will be our fault.

Aine and Debbie watch Murph squealing off in a screech of tyres as another car glides to a stop. John and Paul get out.

"Only a scream away, huh."

Debbie grins. "Well, a very, very long scream."

Aine takes Josie home on the back of her motorbike.

"Mind if I have a fag," Josie says still sitting on the bike. "I can't go in. Not yet. Can't face him."

"You don't have to, you can come and stay in my house, indefinitely."

"What would your mammy think of that?"

"I have my own place."

Shaking the match, Josie takes a deep drag.

"Thanks, but no thanks. I'm not afraid of him or anything, it's just I don't know whether to wipe the floor with him straight away or wait."

Aine laughs, relieved.

"I could kill him, making a holy show of me like that.

Big fool. I was mortified, strutting in there on his little fat feet in his tight jeans, keys dangling. Seen him as others see him. Dyed bloody hair. Even his chest hairs."

Aine giggles.

"No kiddin'. Pathetic. How was I ever afraid of him? How did I let a cretin like that punch me around? Must have rocks in me head."

"Maybe this is your first real opportunity."

"A late developer? But Jeesus, Aine, there's late and late."

"You could have nearly half your life left."

"Yeah, you're right, me ma is over eighty, still going strong. I'm still a young one, what?" Josie chuckles then starts to sing, "You make me feel so young, bells to be rung and a wonderful song to be sung . . . "

"Great voice, husky, sexy."

"Murph's little canary . . . That's what he used to call me. The two kids have good voices, especially Natalie."

"Where are they?"

"England. One nursing, d'other wants to be a footballer."

"Is he good enough?"

"He's great, did his midwifery this year."

"Gotcha!" Josie laughs, watching confusion flit across Aine's face. "Didn't think you'd be into stereotyping. It's me daughter who wants to be a footballer, the son's a nurse, qualified."

"Walked straight into that. If a man said it, I'd jump on him. Think she'll make it?"

"Has the bottle. All she needs is the break. If not, something else'll turn up. Look at me wanting to be a singer and twenty-two years later, painting. Taking to it like I was born to paint. Hundreds of pictures in my head waiting to burst out. I want to paint, paint, paint. Only the coffin lid will stop me."

"Murph?"

"Seen what he's really like. Just a big coward who beat me up to keep me in me place. It's hard to handle, having your eyes opened."

"I'd prefer to go around with my eyes open even if I don't like what I see. Better than having a lout like that closing them for you and I mean literally."

"I know but it's still hard. I was mad about him. He was grand at first, never laid a finger on me for years. Then started picking on me, no reason. I kept the kids and house spotless, went out cleaning. But I couldn't please him. I outsmarted him though. Got me tubes tied after Natalie. Murph couldn't understand why I wasn't gettin' pregnant. I told him the doctor said I was as fertile as a queen bee, could have at least twenty more. He never mentioned it again thinking he must be shooting with blanks. God forgive me."

"Surprised he didn't have it checked out."

"Macho man? You know nothing, Aine."

"You're wicked."

"The only sensible thing I ever did, able to look after the two properly. Gave them a good start. Hadn't a bad childhood. He never touched the kids. A good father. Took out all his frustrations on me . . . The waiting was the worst."

"Sorry?"

"Ye know, between beatings. Almost a relief when he

did it, at least then you could relax for a couple of months. It's a very strange feeling now that I've lost all fear of him."

"It's brilliant."

"It is and it isn't. I've no one to love now that his image is shattered. I've lost . . . "

"The only playboy in the western world."

"More like the only medallion man on the corpo estate."

"You've taken a giant step, become centre stage."

"All because me man tore up me drawings, what?"

"The things that change lives."

"Me granny used to say going to a dance could change your whole life and she was right."

"Yeah, dead right," Aine agrees. "Murph might change too, become a new man."

"Can you see him?"

"It would be a helluva leap for him. Whole new ball game now that you're no longer afraid. The balance of power has shifted. Not in control anymore."

"Could end up my puppet on a string or he could try and beat it out of me."

She drags the last bit of her cigarette and dismounts.

"I'll come in with you."

"No need. Honest. Lookit, Aine, it's all right, I'm not going to bash him, I might damage me hands." Josie laughs, winking at Aine.

"You may become a celebrity for more than fifteen minutes, think you can handle it?"

"Try me." A hint of sparkle in her eyes.

Aine sits waiting. Her heart dropping like a stone.

Josie has been in five minutes, going on six. She imagines she hears thuds. He could be battering her behind the closed door. Should she go in?

The door opens. Murph struts out.

Aine jumps off the bike. Stands ready.

"Would you like a cuppa, Miss?" Murph says, "everything's ready."

"Tea and toast followed by chocolates and flowers," says Josie, eyes screwed up, blowing blue mists of smoke over her spellbound audience next morning at the centre as they gather around her to hear the details.

"Same as after a beating," Nan says.

"Yep, big picture box with a bow on the side, huge bunch of flowers in cellophane while he declared his undying love."

"Till you withdrew the charges," says Nan.

Josie laughs. "Only there are no charges, no bruises, no short-lived power. This time it's the real thing. Afraid of me. Afraid I'll leave him. It's amazing."

"Good on ye, Josie love," Nan says patting her back.

"Now will you lot clear off, I'm only startin'. I've to immortalise Murph in paint before Friday week. Youse have your stuff nearly ready."

"All except me," wails Mary. "I'll never throw a pot properly."

"I told ye, there's only one way, always aim at his head," Nan says. And they crack up laughing.

The sewing women sing as they work. Mary's pots still have a definite tipsy look and she snivels as she moulds.

Aine and Debbie finalise the arrangements for the exhibition in Kilmainham Hospital. Following invitations with phone calls, reminding the press, checking transport.

"Would you look at Murph strutting around the hall like a peacock?" Debbie says to Aine. "If I wasn't a pacifist, I'd hit him. I can just see him grabbing the limelight, getting on chat shows, confessing, purporting to be a new man."

"Forget him. Our little stall is getting all the attention."

"Yes, small is beautiful thanks to Josie."

"Definitely the flavour of the exhibition, the quilt is massive too, real eye-catcher."

"And poor old Mary finally got a bowl finished."

"With a little bit of help from her friendly tutor."

Debbie is not listening. She is distracted by Murph.

"Murph is inching closer and closer to Josie. He'll be in the photograph. Josie's getting uptight. She has enough to contend with without him butting in."

"She looks as if she might punch him."

"Serve him right."

"But it would ruin the exhibition. Take away from her triumph. Imagine the headlines. Finale to Women's Assertiveness Course, Brawl at Exhibition."

"I'll sort him," Debbie says.

"Debbie!" Aine says, filled with alarm.

"It's all right, I'm not going to head butt him."

"Good."

"But I might crush his nuts."

Aine winces.

"Only joking . . . Cross my heart and . . . "

Aine watches as Debbie catches up with Murph and tugs his sleeve. Her big blue eyes shining, her dark curls dancing. She whispers to him, tucking her arm into his and leads him to the drinks. He immediately sucks his stomach to his chest, his little fat feet hardly touching the ground.

Aine joins Josie as a concentration of photographers click and flash at the shocking pictures. An open mouth vomiting chocolates and bits of flowers. A purple penis pumping sperm and pills. Beneath a pulped nose, golden batter pours into a pan flecked with red. Small figures huddle behind a tall green door while a massive boot kicks it in. A tiny hand with scraped knuckles pulls puppet strings. Soft velvet indigo violets shiver with the approach of a huge boot.

"Josephine, is all this personal experience?" a journalist asks.

Josie looks at Aine.

"The ideas came from that ad on the radio," Aine says, "you know the one, 'It's a crime to beat a woman'."

"That picture," Josie says, pointing at 'Behind Closed Doors', that's where it happens. Ninety-nine per cent of woman-battering takes place behind closed doors in the home."

"Are you making a political statement, Josephine?"

"I don't know what a political statement is."

"Did you study art?"

"I left school at fourteen and went into a sewing factory. I never painted. Drew on me copybook at school and got battered by the nun for it. So I stopped."

"The Medusa picture?"

"Medusa who?"

Everyone laughs except Josie.

"What's he on about, Aine?" she whispers to Aine.

"He means the one with the cistern emptying turds into the head."

"But who's Medusa?"

"An aul one with snakes in her hair. Don't worry about it," Aine whispers back.

"All Josie's pictures are original. Not influenced by anyone," Aine says.

"What's next?"

"I want to go on painting."

"Are you full of anger?"

"Yeah I'm bullin' for letting meself be walked on for all those years. I was afraid of me shadow. Never had an opinion. Never knew I could have. Now I've an opinion on everything. Ye can't shut me up."

"Have you a message for the women of Ireland?"

"Yes, do an assertiveness course and come out from behind that green door."

"Could we have a picture of you, Josephine, in front of 'Beaten, Battered and Bewildered'?"

Josie moves and stands in front of the painting.

Aine sees Murph, alone again in the middle of the hall with too many glasses of wine inside him, making him brave, looking as if he desperately wants to proclaim something. Make himself the centre of attention. She advances towards him as Debbie, thin-lipped and definite, approaches him from behind.

136

"All over bar the shouting," Aine says. "I'm sure Josie is exhausted."

"Only for me Josephine wouldn't be painting these picture. She owes it all to me. I am her inspiration," Murph says. His aftershave and hair lacquer blend into a cloying stench.

"Keep a low profile," Debbie whispers to him. "There are hard-nosed feminists over there viewing the paintings. Should hear what they're saying about the bloke who inspired them."

Murph's alcohol-filled eyes roll around the room. They rest on a group of young women.

"They're only kids with Docs and attitude. Poseurs."

"I dare you go over and say, I am the man who battered my wife black and blue, inspiring this painting and want to be recognised for my talent. They'd Bobbitt you on the spot."

"I didn't mean . . . "

"You should have been jailed for what you did to Josie. If I had my way, thugs like you would be put away, never allowed near women and children again. So don't try to become the hero. Wife-beating is vicious, nasty, cowardly and criminal. Josie's pictures should be used in evidence against you."

"I was only . . . "

"I know, trying to steal the limelight. If you have talent other than the fisticuff variety, go and use it and don't try to bury Josie's. Right, sunshine?"

Debbie marches off.

"That's a terrible little girl. Terrible tongue." Tears brimming. "I was only . . . "

137

"Why not show Josie you're proud of her," Aine coaxes, feeling sorry for him. She can't help it.

Murph looks at the floor.

"It's a great achievement and she did it all by herself."

"Don't give me that, youse . . . "

"We provided a service. She did the rest. Josie is special. She has a rare primitive talent."

Murph starts to weep. "I love Josephine. If she leaves me I'll, I'll . . . "

"It's you Josie wants to impress. That's why she was so hurt when you tore . . . "

"It's not fair . . . I've been trying for years. Gettin' nowhere and she comes along, takes up a brush and . . . "

"I know, the Salieri and Mozart syndrome."

"Exactly. I wanted to be the best saxophonist in the country but it's Josie who's going to make it."

He dabs his eyes with an impeccable white hankerchief. "I'm afraid she'll get above herself, leave me."

"I'm sure she doesn't want that. She's very fond of you but if you behave like an asshole, sorry . . . tell her you're proud of her."

Josie comes over. Throws her eyes to heaven.

"Ah come on home, you big baby." Running her arm into his.

He wipes his eyes.

"See ye, Aine," Josie says.

"Thanks, Aine," Murph sniffs.

"Enjoy yourselves."

Over her shoulder Josie says, "We will, we're having a knees-up in our local. You're welcome to come. Murph's playing for me and I'm singing for him. Right, Murph?"

Murph nods.

"Sounds great but I'm wiped out."

"Would you look at that," Debbie says, watching Murph and Josie exit, clamped together. "For better or worse till death do us part. Don't tell me another victim bites the dust."

"Murph's not the worst."

"What! Occasional battering is OK."

"Of course not, but he's trying and, if she'd rather have that than no Murph, who are we . . . "

"We have to show her it's unacceptable."

"She knows that but it's her decision. Our function is to open doors, show the way."

"But the bottom line is, that vicious thug is still bullying, still trying to overshadow her."

"If it suits her to let him share the limelight, it's not for us to judge."

"Share! You mean hog. Talent like hers has to come out. It's our duty to see that it does. When she defied him, we should have helped her give him the push," Debbie says.

"Whether she wants to or not? Big sister knows what's best for you. Trust us."

"Don't be so bloody facetious," Debbie says, her mouth folding in. Her neck muscles throbbing.

139

"Sorry, but I wouldn't like if Josie was more unhappy after being with us than before."

"How can you be such an incurable pessimist? Josie has found she has a wonderful creative outlet. How could that be bad for her?" Debbie asks.

"But who's going to buy the paintings? Who'd want all that sorrow weeping down on them?"

"There you go again, negative, negative, negative. You haven't one positive bone in your body. Good night."

The weeping eye tracks through Aine's dreams. She runs and runs slamming the big green door behind her. Trapping the Eye inside. She wakes whimpering. Wrecked.

"Come in, come in, Aine. I've got the lot," Murph says, pointing to a pile of newspapers, "Some don't do Josie justice, very drawn. We'll have to fatten her up, what?"

"Plenty of loving care from you'd do the trick," Aine says.

"Think so?"

"You're her man. Where is she?"

"Getting up. Thought she should have a lie-in."

"Debbie says sorry," Aine lies.

"Terrible tongue on that young one. Think butter wouldn't melt in her mouth. If my young one used language like that I'd . . . I'd burst . . . I'd give her a good telling off."

Josie staggers in. Aine scrutinises her. Signs of a

hard night, false eyelash stuck in her hair. The other hanging low over her eye. No visible bruising or wounds.

"Me head's opening, get's a cuppa, love."

"Coming up, pet, Aine?"

"Yes please."

"Good night?"

"Brilliant . . . Me and Murph did Johnny Dankworth and Cleo Laine."

"I'd like to have heard that."

"I'd do a turn now only I'm hoarse. Come to check up?"

"That as well as congratulate you, rave reviews, you've done it, Josephine."

"Yeah, I've done it all right, taken Murph's balls."

"He asked for . . . "

"I know and I shouldn't have let him. Should have got help years ago. Anyways it's all behind us, he'll never . . . Poor aul Murph."

Silence as Josie takes a flake of tobacco from her tongue and fills her lungs again with smoke.

"Ready to start on your new project?"

"Lookit Aine, don't get me wrong, it's not as if I'm not grateful or anything but I'm not going to do it. It'd crucify Murph. I thought about it. I need him."

"It doesn't have to be one or the other. Get him to help you. Work as a team."

"What could he do?"

"All sorts of things, get your material ready."

"Dogsbody! He'd love that."

"Agent maybe."

"Ah now Aine, that's pushing it a bit," Josie says, coughing and laughing.

"It's up to you Josie, you know what's best for you. Shame to waste such a wonderful gift, but as I said . . . "

"Poor Murph, he's so insecure. Artane Boys' Band, to army band to playing a few gigs in pubs. Should have stayed in the army. He needs the discipline. The certainty. Not to mention the money. His life was ordered for him. Can't handle the freedom. Still institutionalised. Only march to the one tune."

"Why did he leave?"

"Wanted a new image, heart set on composing a song for Eurovision. Thought he was going to become a rock star, the poor eejit. Grew his hair and all. After a lifetime of short back and sides."

"Not too late for composing anyway."

"Knows nothing about pop music. Can't let it rip, unless he's drunk and then he overdoes it. Too restrained. Too conservative. For feck's sake look at the shine on his cowboy boots. In Artane Industrial School from seven years of age and you know what that was like."

Aine nods.

"And he was one of the lucky ones. In the band. But the things he saw. The brutality. No wonder he wears his pain on his medallion . . . I'm all he's got."

"He could write his memoirs, good therapy. Help him get it out of his system. I'll help him."

Josie says nothing, stubs her cigarette out in the ashtray.

"There's a new programme for men starting in the autumn, Murph might . . . "

"He might and he might not."

"If it were the other way around you'd back him to the hilt."

"Goes without saying."

"Give him the opportunity to do the same for you. Artane, great subject. You could collaborate, that would give him a voice, tell it as it was and you paint it."

Josie fiddles with the butt in the ashtray. "He's got beautiful handwriting."

Aine takes up a photograph of a young boy in blue and red uniform playing a saxophone.

"Boston," Murph says, bringing in a tray.

"Must have quite a story to tell."

"I could write a book."

"Why don't you?"

The phone rings.

"It's ringing all morning," Murph says. "Chat shows and everything. She needs a social secretary."

"Become her manager. You have the discipline. She could paint, you plan."

"Murph is an artist in his own right, a musican, composer. Can't have him running after me," Josie says icily.

"We're in this together, I could make vital contacts."

Murph answers the phone.

"I think you should go, Aine," Josie says, lighting up again and pulling hard on the cigarette.

Aine rides up the mountain and sits at the top of a hill and screams and screams and screams. Frightening the sheep.

Scheherazade 11

❧❧

*D*ervilla Andrews sits. Last night's good time crusted black under her eyes. A glob of golden egg yoke sucks through her night-stained lips.

Mrs Andrews watches the clock scattering minutes all over the place and still Dervilla sits and still her mother stares, pain knotting her chest from held-back words. She would like to hit her daughter. Not a little smack but a hard crack across her smug face. She has felt like that a lot lately.

Dervilla, whom she has spoilt rotten, has her first job interview today and is going to be late. She should let her. Three times she called her before she got up.

"Time," she says hazarding a motherly smile, stopping herself screaming, move your bloody arse. "Yeah, yeah," Dervilla says spooning from the brown shell.

Loitering with no intent whatsoever. She drinks her coffee.

"Brian will be here soon," Mrs Andrews says.

"Get off my case."

"Your father said . . . "

"No he didn't, and if he did, I don't care."

The bell rings, jumping Dervilla. Mascara sheds from under her startled eyes.

"Brian," her mother says.

"Why didn't you call me early."

"I did. Three times."

"Why didn't you make me?"

"I tried."

"What sort of a mother are you? Brian will be livid."

Tough, Mrs Andrews says to herself.

"Do a Scheherazade on him," Dervilla says racing up the stairs.

"Sher who?"

"You know, Scheherazade, the one who tamed the Sultan with her thousand and one stories."

"What sort of story?"

"Your famous one, you know . . . I was that cretin, that should keep him amused."

"I don't know what you mean."

"Your first interview and the bloody tights. I'll be showered and ready before you say summer gold."

"Not ready?" Brian sighs, standing in the kitchen.

"Is she ever?"

He looks at his watch.

"Only got ten minutes. Have to be out of here in ten minutes. Traffic." His leg jigging.

"Her first interview and she's not ready. I was up at dawn for mine. Arrived a half an hour early and that was holding back. Sit down and I'll tell you a story like Scheherazade."

Shock flits across his face but he has lovely manners. He sits.

"Coffee?"

"Please."

148

He pours milk carefully into his cup and sips. "Well then, tell us your story."

"Once upon a time long, long ago . . . "

"A fairy story?"

"Oh no, it's the Gospel truth. The girl in the story is me."

His eyes flick ever so slightly in his well-mannered face.

"Shall I go on?"

"Of course." A hint of a yawn swells his cheeks.

"I'll cut out the frills. The story began in the early sixties, March, nineteen sixty-one, to be precise, when I was going for my first job interview. From the time I got up my mother hadn't stopped advising me, putting me in the picture. Speaking from experience, from one who knows, all that jazz. Answer up, she said. Be enthusiastic. Don't be afraid. All that from one who, over the years, had said shut up, don't be precocious. Don't answer back. And that day a turn-around. I was to shed my chrysalis of muteness and become articulate. Just like that, Mother said. That was bad enough without got-your-hankie-your-letter-your-comb-your-gloves-your-money. I passed the test. She tried harder. Emergency money, she slipped in. I nodded. The second bus, do you know where to get it? She held the question in the air like a trump card. I hesitated. Even have to think for you, she trumpeted. She always did that. Unravelled my thoughts and reknit them, plaining and purling them into a perfect pattern of her own ideas. Whingeing in martyred delight, she got her coat saying she had better come with me. No, I said loud and clear into her face. Wasn't I right?"

Brian nods.

"Dazed, Mother took off her coat and in a strained dishcloth voice said, spend a penny just in case. Equally dazed from my first out loud no, I dutifully went to the bathroom wasting minutes. Then, in a mad rush, I caught the bus but snagged my tights. Not a cute little tear sending little ladders rainbowing demurely down my leg but a big vulgar gash oozing white freckled skin through the navy split. Not a pretty sight."

Scheherazade would have been in deep shit by now, Brian thinks as he tries to manoeuvre his wrist to see the time.

Mrs Andrews sucks long and slow on her cigarette.

"I dragged the alternatives around, sit with the good leg over the bad. Go bare-legged. I sneaked another look at the hairy speckled flesh."

Blushing, Brian squeezes his eyes to blot out the picture.

"New tights was the only answer. Mother thought of everything except spare tights. I would have preferred to break a leg or something. Lie blameless in hospital with my mother fussing over me. Feeling guilty for not coming with me."

"You couldn't bring your mother." A snigger seeps out as he's talking.

"I know that, but I was timid, an only child. And she was a strong woman. Anyway I haven't finished. More coffee?"

"Thank you," he says, resigned.

"I was first off the bus and straight into a chainstore where a little old lady, with a perm screwed into her

150

head like a crown of thorns, pulled and dragged through tights of every shade, black and tan, sunhaze, mink, gunmetal, jasmine, finally swooping delightedly on gaudy summer gold."

"You've a great memory, Mrs Andrews."

"Yes, total recall. I eventually found a large navy pair and careered down to the cash desk, money at the ready and snuck up behind the blue-rinsed head that bobbed and fretted into a large brown handbag and placed my tights beside hers. The assistant bagged both, looking into the distance. I pressed the money into the outstretched hand and was gone before the old lady emerged from her bag."

"You were dead lucky," Brian says, bored out of his tree.

"But that's not all by a long chalk."

That fucking Dervilla, Brian thinks.

"The second bus was packed with shoppers. 'Move along ladies' the conductor said. 'Plenty of room at the front.' I squeezed past the blancmanged bottoms that almost closed the aisle. I was blocked by a real tartar with full blown plastic bags growing out of her arms and a little girl with fat ringlets and red boots holding a shopping trolley. 'Stay where you are Claudia love,' she said standing tough on four inch stiletto heels. Her toes bulging out like purple grapes and her legs bubbling with varicose veins. Her fun-fur bristling."

"Fun-fur?" Brian asked.

"A coat made of rabbit skins. Claudia's red boots didn't budge. Her fat ringlets danced. The conductor slunk upstairs. The pushers behind me stopped and

151

lumped together. I was desperate so I tried to climb over Claudia, the trolley and her mother to the promised seats. The trolley pierced my ankle. The excruciating pain brought me down on Claudia's mother's purple toes. Well the scream was only mighty. I was afraid as well as sorry. 'Bloody culchie' she snapped through her clenched teeth."

"You got off lightly."

"Except the empty seat turned out to be the television seat where the shy shrivelled. You only sat there if you had to or you were a poseur. So I sat mortified, pinned by the curious eyes of the plastic baggers, wishing I had a gaping wound filling the gap in my tights, evoking sympathy instead of the mean interest they showed gawking at the hairy flesh."

Dervilla's mother drags fierce on the dregs of her cigarette.

"Not since Gertie Gallagher stood on my paper dress at the school concert, had I felt so vulnerable. Did I ever tell you about that episode?"

"What?"

"The school concert."

"No." He sighed, looking openly at his watch. "Maybe I should give Dervilla a shout."

"She'll come down when she's ready. Where was I?"

"The school concert," he says, defeated.

"We were fairies dancing around in crepe paper dresses. Then Gertie Gallagher put her big foot on the tail of mine and the whole thing fell to the floor. I can still feel the tug. Hear the tear after all this time. I danced on, petrified in my big navy knickers. The young

152

fellas in the audience came to life, wolf-whistling. The parish priest hurled himself onto the stage, his bog brown face bloated with drink and wobbling with indignation, walloped me off. His peppermint and whiskey breath wheezing purity and chastity and temple of the Holy Ghost into my face, forever fusing the virtues with whiskey and peppermint and cigarettes. Then Sr Theresa, waiting in the wings, swung me by the hair, reefing it out. Still got the bald spot. Look."

She throws forward her hair exposing a small bald patch. Brian politely looks.

"That's desperate, Mrs Andrews."

"It was. I was the laughing stock of the parish. 'Poor Father McAuliffe,' people would say, collapsing into laughter. Poor Father McAuliffe. Nothing about me. I wished him in hell."

"Dervilla's going to be late. Dead late."

"She'll be down in a minute. Where was I?"

"At the concert."

"No, I mean on the bus."

"On the television seat."

God, she's some tulip. By now the Sultan would have topped her. Brian toyed with the idea himself. The bread knife inviting. An end to her story-telling.

"I fiddled with the paper bag, feigning indifference to their stares. I opened it. Summer gold glowed at me."

What in the name of Jasus is she talking about?

"Sorry?" he says politely.

"I had the wrong tights. The little old lady's orange/tan tights. I almost cried, could feel my face trembling. I blamed God. Then remembered I was an agnostic. A closet one, but an agnostic all the same, so I redirected my rage to the stupid girl at the cash desk."

She squeezes her cigarette into her saucer. Lights another. Drags nicotine deep into her lungs and coughs.

Brian makes what he hopes are sympathetic noises, adding, "Terrible experience. Must have felt wrecked."

"Ah but that wasn't the end."

It would be if I had my way, Brian thinks, eyeing the bread knife. He thought his da was long-winded, but Dervilla's ma was something else. All that bloody embroidery. He wonders is it hereditary. Wilde said something about daughters becoming like their mothers.

"The plastic baggers stood as one, gathered their belongings and heaved themselves off the bus. Behind their departing backs, I whisked off the tights, stuck my feet into the new ones and pulled. They stopped over my knees and threatened to slide back down again. I eased forward like a warped plank, squeezing my knees together, ready for the great heave when I caught Claudia's mother's wicked eye on me. Claudia pointing a jeering finger. Her ringlets dancing. I slid back on the sticky vinyl seat."

Off with her head, Brian could hear the Sultan roar.

He pushes his drooping face into an interested expression, cupping it with his hand and leans on the table. She seems glazed in the orange glare of summer gold tights.

"Where was I?"

"On the empty bus hanging on to your wandering tights."

She looks hard at him.

He stands up. "I have to go, I'll be late myself."

"Dervilla'll be very upset, very upset indeed, if you leave her high and dry."

"If she was really interested, she'd be ready by now."

"She's interested, trust me. By the time I've finished the story, she'll be down."

"How long is the story?"

"How long is a piece of string?"

Defeated, he sits back down.

"The bus, now giddily light, gathered speed then suddenly hissed to a stop in utter subjection as the traffic lights glared red. The trolley ladies hobbled alongside the bus. Watching."

"Why didn't you move seats?" His irritation showing.

"Why indeed. Stuck there like a big eejit imprisoned on the television seat. Actually I was waiting for the bus to turn the corner away from prying eyes. The red light was also hindering the shoppers from crossing. Claudia's mother bullied forward into the roaring traffic, daring. Passing cars shaved her fun-fur, skimmed her bulging toes and belched foul fumes into her tight face. Claudia's fat ringlets froze, her mouth opened in a perfect circle and she bawled. Her mother, swearing, retreated to the pavement along with the other plastic baggers who had followed her into the road. I was delighted, God forgive me."

"I thought you were agnostic."

Mrs Andrew's face clotted sourly.

"I haven't finished."

"Sorry."

"The bus lunged forward, lurched around the corner,

roughing along in a drunken high speed, flinging me all over the place, preventing me from pulling up the tights or changing seats. Filling me with anxiety."

Like you're filling me with nicotine and crap, Brian says to himself.

"Long journey," he says.

"Do you want me to stop?"

"No, no, go on, I'm intrigued."

"A herd of schoolboys boarded at the next stop, pushing and shoving, sniffing, dropping pennies, calling to pals, chewing gum rushing down the aisle and surrounding me. 'Hurry up Jacko I've a seat for you,' one fellow shouted as he sat on the outside of the two seater opposite me. Jacko strolled tough and slow down the bus, behind a little old man who elbowed his way into Jacko's seat. He wasn't put together quite right. Know what I mean?"

"Haven't the foggiest," he says. A yawn clearly visible in his voice. No longer caring.

"His legs flared on the wrong camber. Even the cable on his jumper ran a bit off-course. As did his right eye. He glared at me when he meant to glare at the boy beside him who was tittering stupidly. Jacko hung over the pal's seat, his parka jacket crinkling with mischief while his beady eyes hula hooped around the bus looking for victims. He hurled insults at kids who knew better than to answer."

I know the feeling, Brian moans to himself.

"Then Jacko spotted my bulging tights. I squeezed my knees numb. He nudged the pal who was peeling grey chewing gum from his nose and mouth, whispering and snorting into his red ear. The pal's eyes raced to my knees and spluttered and guffawed. Pointing. I was mortified."

"I can imagine."

"The old man's eyes followed. Two pink spots appeared on his cheeks and his eyes one after the other moved to the window. 'Knickers' whispered around the bus. The old man superglued his eyes to the window. His pink spots burning bright."

Like mine at the minute. Brian coughs.

"I couldn't afford to be agnostic any more. Holding on to my wandering tights, I prayed. The bus droned on in snuffles and jeers. Then there was a stampede. A rush of air. I opened my eyes to see the boys halfway down the bus. Jacko turned and shouted, 'Hey miss, get them off ya.' The herd echoed, hooting and hullaballooing. The poor aul fella's lips French pleated. The conductor clattered down the stairs, clipped Jacko's ear saying, 'Shut up ye little gurrier.' He shut up and the rest fell into line. Alighted like angels. The pal's arm around Jacko as he wiped his eyes on his sleeve. I laughed. I also thanked God."

"You did?"

"Well it was a miracle."

"If you say so."

"But that's not all. There was another miracle."

Jeeeesus wept.

"The bus hummed along gathering speed. Passed two stops. The old man jumped up on his ill-matched puritan legs and pressed the bell. As he passed me, the bus lurched, his left foot slapped his right foot, he jerked

157

his hands, grabbed at air and he plonked down on my lap. Shock levelled his hump and co-ordinated his feet. He ran like a whippet down the bus. Was that a miracle or not?"

"Sounds like one."

"I pulled up my tights and prayed summer gold would turn to navy."

"And did they?"

"Are you ready or what?" Dervilla yells, clumping down the stairs. "Stop listening to me ma gassing."

"Did they?"

"Ah now that's another story."

"But Mrs Andrews . . . "

"Come on Brian, I'll be late."

That fellow's too good for Dervilla, Mrs Andrews thinks, lighting up another cigarette.

Skin Deep

❖

I'm watching the road. Afraid to take my eyes off it. He's too close to the car in front. He's muttering.

"What?" I say.

"Just practising, love, getting the feel, the right cadence."

"Cool it, Dad, if you over-practise you won't sound fresh."

"Be prepared, that's my motto," he says. "Which approach is the best, the deep throaty one, the cavalier witty one or the sincere one?"

"Be yourself, relax," I say.

They're all crap. But you have to to be diplomatic. He wants to be in the movies. He's sensitive, or so Mum says and dead keen. Unfortunately he's brutal. It is SO embarrassing. I have on my shades and my hair plaited and hidden under a baseball cap. Hope no one recognises me.

"Dad, Dad, slow down, he's got his right indicator on . . . he's, he's going . . ."

"I see . . . I see," he says sticking his foot to the floor in a screech, throwing me back and forward like a rag doll. I should be in the back.

We were that close I could see the gold hairs on the driver's hands . . . honest.

"That effin' eejit," Dad says honking his horn. He always blames the other driver.

"Don't ask me," I shouted at Mum.

"You have to, he's your father."

"It's a bad time," I said.

She insisted. So I set up the audition. Used my influence. But that wasn't enough. Oh no. She makes me go along to the audition. More a "Go-see" than an audition really. No, not even that, more a "Don't call us, we'll call you" set-up.

"Mind him," she said. "Protect him against himself. He's vulnerable."

"What about me?" I said. "This could ruin me."

"Nonsense," she said.

It's not as if I haven't trouble of my own. I felt a distinct wobble in my front tooth when I woke this morning. I jumped out of bed and looked in the mirror. It looked OK. Carefully sticking my tongue behind it gave a little push. It moved. Slightly. But it moved. I tried again. I felt more than saw. My stomach turned over. I begged God not to let it fall out till after the shoot. It was my big break only a week away on the fifth. Anyone who's anyone auditioned, as well as hundreds of stupid kids who hadn't a clue. I went all out. Would have stood on my head, done anything. And I got it, beating that cow Gabriella Flynn. Just barely. You could say by the skin of my teeth. Which isn't funny now. She was the favourite but lost it overdoing her cute little lisping act. I swung it with my acting. I can really act.

"Cry, Eloise," they say and I cry buckets or have tears running half way down my cheeks or just have my eyes glistening like tear-drenched emeralds. Whatever they ask, I deliver. I modelled myself on Shirley Temple. Now there's a real pro. A natural. I have all her films. I watched her and copied.

"Emulated," Mum says.

Now I do my own thing. Have my own style. And I'm reliable. Never whinge. If I've a headache, stomach ache, I go on. Once even when I was coming down with chicken pox I still carried on. Mum kicked up but I had my reputation to uphold. I've never let them down. That's why when I asked, Sam said he'd see Dad.

As I said Dad wants to be in the movies. Reckons if he's seen in an ad he'll be snatched by Hollywood and be the next Gabriel Byrne. He has this smile. His top lip rolls back from his teeth like a horse and sort of sticks on his gum. And that's his sincere one.

He plastered his face in one thick mass of pan-cake, blotting out his mouth corpse-like. I looked at Mum.

She said, "Let Eloise fix your make-up."

"How did you know I was wearing make-up, Ann?" he asked.

See what I mean? Only let me barely sponge around his lips, giving him back his mouth.

Anyway I do what I have to. Sam the director was very understanding. Said bring Dad along and he'll cure his cough. So I'm sitting in a corner, incognito in my shades and baseball cap, not a hint of red hair showing, watching. The part is already gone of course. They're actually shooting the ad today. Sam said he'd fit Dad in as they're warming up. Roll a bit of film. When Dad sees the video of himself that'll be the hard bit, but you have to be cruel to be kind.

"In and out, fifteen minutes," Sam said. Great. Except we're an hour early. Yep an hour. Dad insisted in case we got stuck in traffic. I'd ask Sam to do him as soon as possible, get it over with, only Sam has trouble with a capital T. The model has a zit on her nose and the whole place is nerve-racked. So I sit and say nothing.

Oh God, there it goes again. It moved. My front tooth moved a bit more. Would the dentist be able to stop it coming, glue it, just a temporary job for a week? I'm afraid I'll wake up one morning and it'll be hanging from a thread, or worse still the tooth fairy will be gone with it leaving a bloody fifty pence piece. This tooth is worth thousands. What's more that bitch Gabriella will get the job. She's the right age and her teeth are like pearls. No hope of them falling out. I'm at that awkward age. Six and a half. Just when my big chances are coming up, my teeth are beginning to rattle. If I lose that tooth, I'm finished. I was a late starter, didn't get into the business till I was three. Gabriella started with her bare bum stuck in the air when she was nine months old. Nappy rash cure. A Page Three of the tots' world. I'm glad I didn't do that myself but still it gave her the advantage of getting into the big ads before her teeth fell out. I'll probably be cute with the gap but when they're neither up nor down, that's a bad time.

I've seen a lot drop by the wayside at that stage and never make it back. Crooked teeth and braces are out. I can't afford to miss this toothpaste ad. Should run for ages, keeping me in the limelight till my second teeth come down. If it falls out before the fifth I'll die. Just die.

"There's a lot of gold in them there freckles," Dad says.

He's right, the freckles make me very marketable and, as well as the tears and smiles, they have now discovered my hidden talent. I can talk as naturally as I can smile or cry. That's why I was chosen. The ad is at least three minutes long, with me saying quite a bit. Hopefully stealing the show from supermodel Petra, the grown-up with full blown adult tantrums. She's the one with the zit today. The ad is for skin cream. Perfect skin naturally required. The male model is deadly, has this earring and the bluest eyes. The way he says "Beauty is in the eye of the beholder and I behold beauty in honey silk skin", makes even toughies like Petra wilt.

Dad would be fine on a voice-over. His voice is dark and creamy, when he's not trying. When he's trying, it goes up and up sing-songy, hills and dales. It's not fair putting me under this pressure. At this very moment I could even be past my sell-by date. I should be at the dentist getting advice instead of watching him making a fool of himself, going up to women saying his lines. Some of them laugh, like the old lady with skin like a crumpled paper bag.

His latest victims are two models with long blonde hair. They give little skips and tinkle like bells when he says his bit. I really can't take it anymore so I slide along to the ladies and sit in tight to the wall and watch women doll themselves up. The two blondes fall in the door, cross-legged, cracking up, can't say anything till they come out of the loos. Seemingly Dad went up to Petra and did his spiel. Which might have been harmless enough, except for the zit and his timing.

As I said, she was freaking out with this massive pimple on her nose. She had squeezed it and her make-up lady had camouflaged it brilliantly and everything seemed OK until it started to weep. And Sam said he was sorry but it wasn't good enough. Petra was flouncing out when Dad cornered her and said his bit. She kneed him. My heart zigzagged across my chest. God, Petra'll destroy me if she finds out I'm related to him, claim I put him up to it. She hates me already, heard her saying to Sam I was a precocious little bitch. I creep out sticking to the wall bungee like. Check the place for Petra's mates. Dad is sitting sort of hunched over. He is the most beautiful colour. It's trans . . . transluc . . . you now sort of see-through, between a yellow and sage green and the pain on his face is so acute, so sincere it would have been perfect for a pain killing ad.

"Dad," I whisper when I'm certain the coast is absolutely clear. He looks up, slipping on his sincere mask, his lip peels back to his gum and he begins:

"Beauty is in the eye of the beholder and I behold . . . "

I tense up, grinding my teeth, feel the crack and taste blood in my mouth.

I start screaming.

The Square of the Extinct

We waited for Dad at the airport glowing with expectation. I was almost thirteen. He arrived. Blond hair, golden skin, blue eyes, bearing gifts.

"My girls," he exclaimed scooping us up. His smile melting the onlookers and us. Mum all smiles and hugs. A week later they separated.

Something happened after we had finished the croissants and ignored the fois gras. I knew by her voice something was wrong. It was rising in cracked arpeggios. Been rising for days. I don't think it had anything to do with the fois gras although Mum said she couldn't eat such a thing knowing what they did to the poor geese. Dad had a hunted look.

On the sixth day I awoke to the sound of nothing. The sky was a nothing colour. Mum was a nothing colour. Her hair stood up in spikes like it had a bad night.

"Where's Dad?"

"Gone. Left."

My head was clunking. My mouth cranking to get words out. Nothing came.

"We're splitting," she said, her split ends nodding in agreement.

169

I felt my head splitting in two. My brain splattering to one side. Then the other. Tumbling me around.

"But why?" I asked this mousy plain woman. "You don't fight or anything. He's perfect, ask anyone."

All my mates fancied him. Every single one of them. Especially Michele who spoke to him with her nipples. She was the first to sprout and was always showing off.

Mum cackled and drew deep on her cigarette.

"Yes, he is gorgeous. He has the most beautiful hands. Everyone laughs when I say that. Singling out his hands, when he is beautiful all over."

"Why then?"

"He used me. Deceived me. I'll never, ever, forgive him."

I could smell the bitterness in the tail end of the smoke she puffed out.

Mum's mates came around, filling the house. Covering the silence with whispered outrage. But the house still gaped with his absence.

"Pas devant l'enfant," Aunt Harriet signalled when I appeared as they bad-mouthed Dad.

Shut the fuck up, I wanted to scream at them.

"Annulled!" Gran screamed, wrapping my heart in barbed wire. "Nobody in our family ever had a marriage annulled," she said, her jaw jerking to the click of her knitting needles. Her long elegant fingers caressing the wool. Ribbing a jumper for Dad. Knit one purl one. The jumper he'll only wear when visiting her.

"No marriage existed! Did you ever hear the like. What about you, pet. Do you not exist either?"

Clickety click. "A full-blooded man like that. Should be down on her knees thanking God for such a husband. If she tried a bit harder. Made an effort. 'Definitely no oil painting,' your grandfather, God rest him, said when Matthew brought her home. No bum, belly or bust." Clickety click. "A matchstick. His 'Lowry girl' Matthew called her . . . A golden man. In that awful bedsit. Cold and damp. My heart is dead. Don't know how I'm functioning," Gran said shrinking into her baggy flesh.

I hated my mother.

"My goodness you are a big girl," my father said once when I was fifteen and blubby. Mum went for him. "She's perfect. She is what I always wanted to be."

He held out his hands, palms up. "Sorry, sorry, afraid she'd fall into flab, my genes." Patting his fattening stomach.

I stopped eating chocolate and crisps. Did a bit of exercise. I'd do anything for him.

"Agadir for Christmas." My mother shuddered. "Why not Austria or somewhere more Christmassy?"

"Postcard version?" I said, my curled lip sticking to my gum.

"I mean somewhere that celebrates it. Somewhere with character. Agadir's new. I'm surprised at your father."

"Beats Kerry, turf fires pissing rain and the stench of poor mutilated turkeys."

"Well you'll get plenty of cous-cous in Agadir. Not a

171

lot of culture in that pile of rocks though. Rubble bulldozed into a man-made mountain." She sniggered.

"Sun, sea and sand is all I want," I hissed.

"Just as well, that's all it adds up to."

I left out the fourth S, sex. The one I wanted most. A romantic tryst with a wild man of the East.

"Men . . . " Mum fudged. "Moroccans are mad for young blonde girls. And are very handsome and persuasive."

"How would you know, you've never been?"

"The girls have."

Girls! I stifled a snort. Aul wans with sprouting chins, especially Aunt Harriet. She who encouraged Mum to throw Dad out. And when Mum nearly took him back she was there all the time. Making sure. Even when I pleaded.

"The souks," I said, "I'm really looking forward to them."

"You were always into markets."

"Yeah, remember the Dandelion."

"Do I what. You gave me candles every Christmas, birthday and Mother's day."

"You said you liked them," I said, defensive.

"Oh I did, I really did. Best presents ever."

The Dandelion was Dad's and my favourite place when Mum and he split up.

"Where'll we go, princess?" Dad'd ask when he came to collect me.

"The Dandelion," I'd say. Always the Dandelion. Dad's friend, Peter, had a stall there. Made the most incredible candles.

"Well, I don't intend being promiscuous if that's what you're implying," I said, throwing Mum into denial.

"I never." She sighed her dutiful sigh.

"You take good care of her, Matthew," Mum warned Dad. "Nothing to mar the holiday."

"Best behaviour. Promise."

"No leaving her alone." Her antennae tingling.

"I'll chaperone her everywhere."

"Mum, I'm not a kid, I'm eighteen," I whinged.

"All the more reason."

"Kerry again?" he asked smiling. "Plenty of mountainy men."

She turned coy. They were really good friends now. Almost best friends. She told him everything.

Dad was true to his promise. Never let me out of his sight. And we were staying at this crappy apartment off the beaten track. Rough area. No night life. No blokes. Not even a room with a view. The Kerry mist, crowded pubs and the craic seemed almost cool.

"Is this it?" I whined on the warm Moroccan air on the fourth day. Dad, lying by the pool, oiled and tanning nicely, being ogled by the German woman, sat up startled.

"I didn't realise you were bored," he said, looking genuinely sorry.

"Out of my tree. I'm sick of souks, spices and swimming pools and not a single offer of even one camel for me. Do you realise the most amazing thing I've seen in three days is that gross woman in electric pink bicycle shorts moulded into her fat stomach and bum."

173

"The pink lady." Dad winced. "Makes my teeth water."

"It's all right for you, you have your frau."

"She's practising her English."

"And the rest."

"Actually I'm finding her quite intrusive. Hardly read a word today and the husband is giving me funny looks."

"I'd say she has a case to answer."

"Where'll we go, princess? Entirely at your disposal," Dad said, getting up.

We took a blue taxi to the beach and enter another world. Sugar white sand, miles of it and happy people enjoying themselves. We swam and sunbathed. I feasted on the gorgeous hunks playing ball on the beach. I rated them one to ten. None less than seven and a half.

We strolled along the sea front and came across a tented village. Wonderful crafts. Like Aladdin's caves.

"I am Berber," a boy, leaning on a rope, his leg swinging to the limit like a pendulum, said.

"Everyone's a Berber," Dad bantered.

"Truly I am. I come from the mountains. I am Mohammed. Abdul is Berber, too," he said pointing at the bent head of the craftsman. Raven hair glinting metallic blue in the sunlight as he delicately threaded silver wire with beautiful sand-brown hands.

"I will give you a thousand camels for her," Mohammed said.

"Too little and too young," Dad said.

"I like older women," he said.

Dad and I cracked up. Abdul raised his head. I saw

his face. It was the most amazing face I'd ever seen. Glittering black eyes and perfect white teeth. I picked up rings, black entwined with silver. I held out my hand and he slipped one on each finger sending shock waves through me.

"That one," I said, "no, that one . . . " Stalling, keeping his hand on mine. Asking questions so he looked into my eyes, a breath away. Could he hear my heart? See it hopping through my light dress. He turned to my father, asking him his opinion. Charming him. Good move. Dad became engrossed. Took over. Moving into my space. My hand was dropped in favour of a flamingo about a metre high with splayed feet. Abdul explained the design intricately woven with silver wire into the metal.

"Dad, Mum wants copper trinkets, they're on the next stall," I said desperately trying to get rid of him. The words bounced off his unresponsive back.

"Dad!" I shouted peevishly. He turned, surprised. Like he'd forgotten me. He went reluctantly. I bought a ring for each finger. Threaded in silver, made by Abdul's hands. And a bracelet.

"We'll come back to the beach tomorrow," I said as we stroll back to the apartment. "I fancy the flamingo."

Dad chortled. "Abdul is beautiful but it's not on. I promised Fran."

"Only looking," I said.

"If I believed that . . . "

I felt a sulk forming at my lips. " Did I ask for anything?" I snapped.

"Yes, a flamingo."

175

I laughed, linking my arm through his.

"Let's eat French tonight for a change," he said.

"If we can get past Ahmed."

Ahmed was cajoling tourists into his restaurant in six languages as we snuck past. The French place was dull. The meal disappointing. Cold. And we missed the buzz of Ahmed's.

"Sucked diesel, eh?" Ahmed said, the tassel on his fez shaking with laughter as he spotted us on our way back.

"Indeed we did," Dad admitted. "You are indeed the best."

"Oiche mhait," Ahmed said.

I dreamt of Abdul. His beautiful hands, face, hair. I woke in a fever. It was up to me to make the move. I'd ask him out. One night. One hour. Anything. Maybe even ask him over to Ireland for a holiday. I could come back on holiday without Dad.

I stood unseeing at the sea front while crowds hustled around. Pain, real and immediate, coursed through me like a fan of broken fingers. Abdul had gone. The tents gone. Like they'd never been. A mirage.

"When are we going to Marrakech?" I asked Dad when I discovered that's where they'd gone. Only in Agadir for the arts festival.

"Tomorrow, I've already booked." He beamed.

I hugged him tight, telling him he was the best, like when I was a kid.

"Let's go shopping. Get some gear for the trip."

"Essence of comfort. Don't know why they're not worn more," Dad said trying on a sage-green jellaba. So him. I could just see him lounging in it in his

176

amazing new apartment in Temple Bar. All steel and glass. My jellaba was midnight blue with a veil to match.

"Early to bed. Six in the morning," Dad said. He went out for milk. He was away for ages. The German woman waylaid him, he said. Chatted him up.

She was on the the bus to Marrakech, husbandless. The pink lady was there too. Though this time skirted in pink. We stopped high in the Atlas mountains. I fiddled with jewellery. Not interested. Anxious to get away. The German woman asked Dad's opinion. They pored over beads and bangles. He fastened necklaces around her bent neck. Closed bracelets on her gold-tanned wrist. She bought.

I noted, with pumping heart, the tents on the edge as we came into the pink city.

All morning we were shunted through palaces and posh places, the German woman smiling permanently in our direction. Taking photos of us. Of me. Of Dad. I offered to take one of her at the tombs of the Saladins. She declined. Dad offered five minutes later. She lit up like a neon bulb and posed under an orange tree. She was a good-looking woman. About Dad's age. They made a lovely couple.

"Do you want to sit with her?" I asked, hoping.

"No, definitely not," he said.

Dad's a coward when pursued. Mum was always rescuing him from predatory females.

We were bussed out of the city for a lunch of couscous. Entertained by dancers in traditional costume. My mind toiling. How to get away. The souks, my only chance. But Dad would go spare.

"I'm going to slip off to La Mamounia," Dad said as we hissed to a stop in Djemma El f'na. The Square of the Extinct.

"What?"

"La Mamounia, stunning place. Winston Churchill's favourite watering hole. Even named the piano bar after him."

"Sounds gross."

"It's a fine marriage of Art Deco and Moorish. Magnificent filigree."

"I'm not going."

The guide will take care of you. I've already asked."

He was dumping me. Shock changed to delight in a second.

"Stay with the tour. Meet you back here at six."

"Change of plan," I told the guide as he herded the tourists into the warren of souks. "I'm going with my Dad," I said on the hoof.

He legged it after me. I slipped into a doorway. He called to Dad who was getting into a taxi. Dad turned and waved. The guide took the wave as affirmation. Relief smoothing his brow, he disappeared into the souks.

Hooded and veiled, I walked towards the tents on the fringe. It was farther than I thought. I arrived hot and sticky. Hyper. The flamingo. I saw the flamingo. Bracelets, rings threaded in silver. Tools, everything, but no Abdul. Cool it, I told myself but I was in overdrive. Mohammed was chatting up tourists. I hovered. Moved away. Bought mint tea. Examined the goods in every tent from cedarwood to rugs and everything else under the sun. I wandered back. Paused at the cool copper at the next stall. Watched. Dad would go spare if he knew. Still no sign of Abdul. I moved to his stall.

"I am Berber, I make all these," Mohammed was saying to two pretty American women. "My assistant is gone for the day but my friend and I will meet you later. Give you a nice time. My friend over there, see." He pointed.

A boy, sixteen at the most, grinned cheekily over the copper pots. The women, thirty something, jammed their jaws together in suppressed laughter.

"I give you bargains. These rings made by my own hands. Try them on."

They examined the rings.

"Gifts . . . one each."

They took the rings and went in a cross-legged titter. Mohammed cursed.

I rubbed the flamingo.

"Abdul?" I said taking down my hood and removing my veil, throwing him into recognition.

"He is away." Cold. Defensive. Hostile. He rearranges the rings.

"Tell Abdul . . . " I felt the heat rising in my face. The stall rocked and swayed before me. Despair lapping behind my eyes, about to gush. He stopped sorting. Looked up. Saw.

179

A smirk budded in his eyes and flashed on his lips. Cockiness regained.

"When will he be back?"

"Tomorrow."

Get a grip, I told myself. For fuck's sake get a grip.

"Gone to see a man about a dog," he drawled.

He shouted to his mate in Arabic. No doubt deriding the stupid tourist with the hots for Abdul. Punishing me for witnessing his humiliation. Giving away his master's goods to no avail. His mate pumped his arm in reply.

"My friend will help you out."

I walked away hooded and veiled against the jeers that followed me. Tears plopped. The wet veil clung to my nose and mouth. The muezzin was calling the people to prayer. The sun had already dropped behind the hill. The Square of the Extinct ghosted in plumes of white smoke, rising like incense from the food stalls in the dusky light. I wanted to display Mohammed's severed head.

Swirling throngs good-humouredly jostled, enjoying the circus of snake charmers, acrobats, dancers, fire-eaters. I boarded the bus parked outside tea rooms, my face stiff with dried tears. Everyone was there except Dad. The German woman's forlorn face dragged with disappointment. The rest showed their purchases. Relived the afternoon. Voices lifting and dropping. Camels' fierce bad breath. Foul tempers too. Like sitting on an orange box. The knack is to sit legs out front like the Berbers. That's no sixteenth century dagger, sonny, that's a bit of electric conduit pipe. Guffaws. Could murder a plate of chips. Hope it's not that bloody semolina again. Who's missing? That big chap, the one gone native in that roby thing. Ah yes, Mr Smoothie. Always joking with the guide and driver. Shush. The pink lady nodded in my direction. No offence.

The bus was purring, ready to take off. The driver and guide looked questioningly in my direction. I fastened my eyes to the window.

I saw Abdul. I thought I saw Abdul. I blinked twice, three times. He was there. Illuminated in a corridor of light. Definitely him. Dad was with him, arm around Abdul's shoulder. Dad had found Abdul for me. My heart zig-zagged. I half rose.

Dad's fingers fondled Abdul's neck. Then lips on lips. The bus was revving. A mewl burst from me.

"Don't worry, love," the pink lady said, "we won't go without your daddy. Hold your horses," she shouted to the driver, "there's one more to come."

"If it were you or me they'd have gone without us. Fifteen bloody minutes over," her husband barked.

"Shut up you, can't you see she's upset?"

I bunched up. Go, I want to say, please go. Don't look. Don't see.

Dad was there. His beautiful hands flat against the pane. The bus sighed open and scooped him up and we were away. His sincere smile, full of apologies, smoothing his way down the bus. Caressing each one with his eyes. Warming them into sympathy. Lost and is found. They're only short of cheering. Mr Smoothie.

He looked at me. Crunched tight to cracking point. My fists like adders' heads. His face shuffled like a pack of cards. King, Queen, Knave. All of them.

Tompkins Square Park

"OK, lady," the men said when I explained from behind the closed apartment door that I couldn't let them in, because I was only a guest there.

When they came back, banging on the door, shouting, "Open up, lady," fear buzzed in my head like a trapped bluebottle, churning up the chef, the ballet dancer and the soup. Taking my breath away.

I awoke shivering on the floor. The men gone. I took my coat and left.

Lucky . . . lucky . . . lucky . . . I said it like a mantra. As I rocked back and forth. Back and forth. In my big navy coat. On the park bench. Me and the Indian. He didn't rock. He didn't do anything. Just sat. His Big-Chief headdress was stubby and broken. His stoic face bruised purple on one side. When not battered, he had the palest face. Always in the park or on the edge. Always alone. Always immaculate in his Indian gear. Until today that is. Not his day either.

Or the grey bearded man in the silky green dress, clinging to his legs above heavy boots. A matching

185

green silk ribbon tied back his seaweedy hair. He rooted in the bins, getting nothing.

Did the Indian eat the soup?

Did the old man in the green dress eat it?

The soup was always on my mind. The soup, the chef and the ballet dancer. The chef lived on the next block with the ballet dancer. I used to pass their apartment every day. He made soup for the down-and-outs in the park. Good soup they said. Last time he made it, he used the ballet dancer's head. His friend testified. Saw the head in the pot. I nightmared about him and the Hispanic.

The Hispanic waiting for me. Waiting to get me. Like the American on the plane said he would.

"Some day," he said, "you'll be standing on the corner and this Hispanic will come along and slice your head off. No reason. Just 'cause you're there." Then he smiled his good clean all American smile and said, "Have a nice day."

I told Mick and Una and they fell about laughing. Told all their friends. But I knew he was out there, waiting . . . I always had my key out, ready . . . nearly always tore the skin off my knuckles trying to get it into the lock, fast. Always fumbled.

I'd seen him on the corner. Waiting. I showed Mick. He said he was a fellow from Mayo waiting for a lift. Mick's always tried to console me. What'd he say about today?

Those men trying to break into the apartment. Beating down the door till I couldn't breathe. He'd make an excuse for them, just like Una. And they'd look at each other. And Una would have her "It's her or me", look.

I came for a few weeks, till I got my bearings, armed with tea and chocs and crisps. And stayed and stayed. The tea and chocs and crisps were long gone. I clung like film to Mick and Una was pissed off. Poor Mick was torn.

Can't throw out his poor little cousin, now can he?

Una hated me. I hated me. A cringing eejit. At first I was a joke. Then a burden. An intolerable burden. I caused rows. I heard them. Una saying things like, paranoid and unsuitable and not cut-out and asking for it.

"Asking for what?" he jumped in.

"To be mugged, raped, or murdered or all three."

He said he'd never thought he'd ever hear a fully fledged feminist like her saying such a thing. Una exploded with, "She's so terrified, she's a pushover, she freezes if anyone looks at her."

He said coldly, "So she's vulnerable and needs to be taken care of and you want me to throw her to the wolves?"

And she said in her last-straw-voice, "*Send her home*."

Home, I wanted to go home more than anything else, but what could I do?

"A Donnelly visa," they said, "You lucky, lucky thing." I hugged myself with the excitement of it all. Da kept

187

singing "New York, New York," when he wasn't humming "Manhattan".

"Say hello to Delancey Street for me," he said. And I did.

When the train pulled in at Delancey, Una shouted, "Hold your nose and run for it." I ran past the homeless, the junkies, the beggars with their white plastic cups meekly uttering "change". The pong of urine and sweat followed me into derelict Delancey.

I never mentioned Delancey Street when I wrote home. Instead I eulogised about Una's super job with the fab freebies. How she brought to me to see Steffi Graf in Madison Square Gardens, best seats too, and the black-tie-invitation-only painting exhibitions, where the glitterati rolled up in their chauffeur driven limousines. Never a mench of the homeless, rolled up in sleeping bags in adjacent doorways.

So now I was trapped in my big navy coat. In Tompkins Square Park. In my invented landscape.

Una came in her power suit with massive shoulder pads. She stood before me in her "no-nonsense" stance. Stabbing the lean earth with her stiletto heel.

"So here you are, Siobhan, you do surprise me. Here of all places, who'd have believed it? Won't Mick be amazed?"

I rocked faster.

"Stop that stupid rocking and listen to me, listen to me, you silly cow, the men trying to get into the apartment were from the cable company, the *Telephone Company*."

I tittered. She lost her cool. Her mouth opened and words poured out, spilling all over the place like coins from a slot machine jackpot. All the things she wanted to call me and couldn't while Mick was around. The titters multiplied into hysterical laughter and I rocked so hard I was almost in a spin. She backed away slowly. I slowed down to a steady rock. I was no longer laughing.

She was right about the park. It was ludicrous. On our doorstep, and I'd never been in it before now. Even when Mick tried to inveigle me in to play basketball, I wouldn't budge. I observed it daily from the safety of the apartment. Sat on a high stool with my coffee and bagels and watched the children flying high on swings, the joggers, the basketball players, the Ukrainians playing chess. The sanitised view. I knew if I moved my eyes slightly to the left I'd see *Them*. The crackheads, drunks, down-and-outs, lolling on benches or in sinister groups. And maybe even the Hispanic waiting for me.

Now, the park was my refuge. I had to laugh and laugh.

Mick gathered me up and carried me back to the apartment. He held my hands. I watched them shake as if they belonged to someone else.

"You've got to write to your mother," he said. "Tell her how you feel, how unhappy you are, that you want to go home."

189

A hairline crack in his voice. His hands tightened. His beard was sprouting little gold needles. A sliver of tomato was caught in his tooth.

Una said "I'll get pen and paper." Her face pleated in satisfaction.

"Auntie Kate'll understand," Mick said.

I laughed to myself at the thought of my mother, understanding. Especially after all the boasting she did to mothers of illegals.

"Of course," she crowed, "our Siobhan has a green card, can do what she likes, go where she wants. Get a well paid job." Just stopping short of saying, "Not like your lot."

I can see them accosting her on my return.

"See your Siobhan's home."

"Holiday," she'd brazen.

"So soon?"

"Can come and go as she pleases."

"Looks peaky."

"You know these high flying executives." She'd laugh her woman-of-the world laugh.

"When is she going back?" they'd slip in. Slyly.

"Soon, very soon," she'd snap, "*and*, she's taking Sean back with her."

"Sean?" I said, on a wave of tears.

"Ah yes, Sean," Mick said, "can't be helped."

"I'm his saviour."

"I wouldn't go as far as that." He smiled sadly.

"His ticket to America."

"I know, but you can't sacrifice yourself. No one would expect . . . "

"Mam . . . "

My tears splashed on our hands. Mick's Adam's apple bobbled up and down. His eyes misted. He retreated into our childhood, drawing me into the garden where the Cordylions grew . . . the strawberries holed by worms . . . the pet jackdaw . . . Superman's medicine exploding, skin hanging in bubbles . . . I peered into the spaces in his conversation. He shifted uncomfortably in my silence.

"Pen and paper," Una said.

"Just a note," Mick said, steering me towards the table. "Tell her about today . . . the park . . . "

I nodded and sat.

"A few words'll do," Mick encouraged.

Una prattled on saying things like, "Tell them I was asking for them". Mick kept giving her "shut-up" looks. But she was so relieved at my pending exit, she couldn't.

Mick said, "Cut it, Una." And she did.

I saw their faces, Mam's, Dad's and Sean's. Mam's loomed large. I started writing.

Dear Mam, Dad, Sean,

Eat your hearts out, you poor suckers, stuck in murky, misty, rheumy Irish November. Here in the Big Apple the air is crunchy crisp. A bright, glittery, glossy sort of day. In the park opposite, pure yellow leaves flutter to the ground making a sun carpet.

Da, you'll never believe this, Charlie Parker,

Charlie "Bird" Parker lived on the far side of the park, just across the street. When you come over you'll see the plaque.

The bad news. I think Mick and Una are about to split up. They fight all the time.

Love Siobhan.

PS We're out of tea bags.

Warrior Queen

✣

"*I* should have bought that gun in Philly," my mother's tinny voice quivered over my shoulder. "We're all going to be murdered."

"You're not helping," I said, cutting sickles of pain into my palms with my nails.

"We should have stayed on the highway. There's bound to be a filling station."

She was right. Dead right. It was midnight. Four cream-puff visitors in a white rented car, almost out of petrol in a no-go area of New Jersey. A black black night. No lighting. Metal innards, prized and twisted, hang loose from smashed street lights. Not a sound except a can stuttering and stumbling in the wind. The seediest place. You could smell the poverty. Raddled hookers on the corners. Dereliction flickering in candle lit dilapidated buildings.

"Crackhouses," Kim said. Kim, who was reared in the projects, knew.

"I should have bought the gun in Philly," my mother said.

"We weren't in Phila-bleeding-delphia," I said choking her off.

"Wherever, it makes no difference, I should have bought it anyway," Mother said, affronted.

A pain shooting up my temple began corkscrewing across my brow.

"Maebh's uptight," Izzy, the true blue American Wasp, consoled my mother.

"She's no right getting shirty with me just because she put us in mortal danger."

"Pay no heed," Izzy whimpered.

Maebh would like to scream – it's all your fault, Izzy. This trip was your idea.

"Show your mother Amish country before she leaves," Izzy suggested. "She'll love it. Good clean living. Wholesome as American pie."

And we did. And bloody ungrateful she was too.

"I suppose it would have been nice if it wasn't closed," Mum said. "All that way just to see a horse and cart disappear into the sunset."

The day started with delay. The car hire firm wouldn't give me the car because I hadn't enough money in my account to cover accident. I had to ring Mum and tell her to come and bring her credit card with her. She went into spasm.

"I couldn't go on the subway. Don't ask me. I'd get the wrong train." She puffed and snorted.

"Grab a cab," I said and gave directions.

She arrived, pecan-faced, clutching her credit card and directions written in lipstick on the edge of a newspaper. Her legs swooning.

"I had to keep telling the cabdriver the street.

Spelling it out to him. He hadn't a clue. Hardly spoke English. Only arrived from India last week. We had to count the streets. Imagine!"

Yeah, yeah, yeah, I wanted to say but said instead, "Sorry Mum."

So we hired the car. With her still whingeing in my ear, I drove on the wrong side of the street. I do not know how I did it, but I did. She told me. Her head in a steel tilt. Her lips folded inwards. Clucking and tutting.

Then Kim was late. Really late. Her phone engaged. Izzy and I took turns ringing her buzzer to no avail.

The day rushed past in a whirr of yellow cabs and cop sirens as we sat outside Kim's apartment, Mum giving a running commentary on the sleaze and filth of crusties living on the sidewalk. Eventually hunger drove her out of the car to buy a bagel.

"I had to pick my steps around a man wrapped in his duvet propped up with pillows, eating breakfast. His dog beside him. It was like walking through someone's bedroom. Very embarrassing," she said settling down in the back seat to eat her sesame seed bagel. Almost a hundred dollar bagel as it turned out. She had paid for it with a hundred dollar bill and got the change of five. We didn't discover this until hours later.

Around noon, eyes hooded in wads of sleep, Kim came out. She'd had a visit from the cops at five in the morning. Kicked open her apartment door brandishing guns, NYPD blues style, looking for some drug dealer. Wrong apartment, wrong building even. The janitor said he kept telling them. So poor old Kim fell into a deep sleep and the cat had knocked the phone off the hook.

"Sue them," Mum screamed, raging more for herself than for Kim.

"They apologised and will pay for the door," Kim yawned.

"That's not good enough," Mum said even though she had had her photograph taken with cops outside the ninth precinct where they shoot NYPD Blues and praised them to the heights, telling them they were better than the series.

"I was expecting Jersey cows and pasture land," Mum said as we emerged from the Holland tunnel into the thick of industrial Jersey. Her eyes dusted in disappointment.

In the thick of traffic on the cluttered highway, I had to change lanes, cut across a juggernaut. Later he sideswiped me, making me slam on, throwing everyone forward. Mum took out her rosary beads.

A blast of chilled air froze the sweat bubbles as we entered a restaurant about two hours later.

"Unnatural, flying in the face of God. I'd rather be hot and sticky. Vest, you need a vest," Mum said, shivering at Izzy's bare midriff.

The blast of cold air from the air conditioning was nothing to the frost that descended when she discovered she had been short-changed with her bagel.

"They all look the same," she said, looking at the dollar notes. "Same size, same colour. It's not right."

"I didn't know your mother had a charisma bypass," Kim said licking her spoon clean.

"More a genetic disorder, my grandmother was the same. I take after my daddy."

"Your daddy must be having a real nice time," Kim said.

We arrived in Amish country when they were going to bed. Well, not exactly bed, but everywhere was locked up. And nearly everyone gone home. There was one souvenir shop open. Selling mostly stuff made in Taiwan. We bought a bag of peas in their pods from girls in white bonnets and blue dresses and sneakers. Sitting by the roadside, cracking open the pods, we saw the girls get into a big Chevvie and drive off in a spiral of dust.

"We should have done the Hershey chocolate tour instead. At least we'd have been sure of a Hershey bar," Mum bleated.

I was really grateful to Kim for not saying what she thought.

We stopped on our way back at a roadside cafe.

Mum criticised everything from the chicken to the salad.

Now midnight, looking for a gas station in a no-go area.

"There are places in Dublin I wouldn't go even in daytime. We're going to be murdered," Mum said.

"One way or another," I hissed.

I knew, if and when my mother got home, she'd tell everyone. Badmouth me. The only thing she'd remember about the trip was being lost in the ghetto.

"Wait till your father hears about this," she warned.

Maebh imagined her father lying on the couch watching football on the television as the wail of his wife washed over him. His eyes flickering past her to the screen as he grunted sympathy.

"Maebh, I called her, after the warrior queen," her mother told Izzy. "I don't know why." Implying great disappointment.

Izzy began to babble on the cusp of hysteria.

"Cool it, Izzy." Kim said.

And she did.

"Hail Mary full of grace, the Lord is with thee . . . " Her mother intoned, rattling her rosary beads with Izzy bleating amens from under her sheet of blond hair.

"Look, look up there, there's a gas station on the corner," Kim said. "And it's open."

We yowled with relief.

"Thank God, thank God and his blessed Mother," Mum said.

I turned the car on to the forecourt. All eyes swivelled towards us.

"What's a whitey like you doing in a place like this?" A girl whispered as I queued to pay. Her face shining almost blue black.

"Getting gas," I said. Fear coming in a rash.

"You in deep shit. Those skinny celery sticks of legs can hardly hold you up."

My legs waved in response. Would they even carry me back to the car?

I looked towards the car. Three white faces ghosted the windows. The girl's words verified what Kim said, what I knew in my heart. We were in crack country and I still had to drive back through those streets to get back on the highway.

"Mind how you go. There's a lot of crazies around here," she said kindly.

And there were. I could see them all around.

Back in the car I revved hard. Too hard. Foot stuck on the gas. I couldn't stop myself. Fumes. Stall.

Knuckles, topped in silver and gold, tap on the window. Arms tattooed, scarified and branded. Nose, ears and eyebrow ringed. Neck wide as his skull.

"Don't open the window," Mum ordered. "He's like something out of *National Geographic*."

He was straight out of Mad Max, I thought but didn't say as everyone rushed to shut Mum up. Hissing and elbowing her.

I rolled down the window.

"You guys musta been using the best detergent, y'all whiter than white."

Pearly teeth wrap around a barrel laugh.

Izzy, Kim and I laughed long and scared.

"You need to get your ass outa here real quick."

"I've flooded the engine."

"I'll give you a push."

"Do you want us to get out?" Kim asked.

"No need."

He pushed. The car started.

"I should have bought that gun in Philly."

I turned and looked at her. Her face was reduced to bone and lines. Her grey roots growing by the minute.

"You're dead right," I said.

"Hail holy Queen, Mother of . . . "

The man appeared at the window.

God, please keep my mother's mouth shut, I prayed.

"Now lock your doors and follow me," he said. "Don't stop even if the lights are red."

He moved over to his four-wheel and got in.

"He's luring us to our death," Mum said.

I followed his jeep, reinforced with bull bars. It was our only hope.

"You should have bought that gun in Philly," Izzy whispered on the edge of hysteria.

I drove past the crackheads, over broken glass, looking straight ahead. Conscious of being watched and resented. And ripe for plucking. Suddenly the lights of the highway glimmered. The jeep pulled over. A hand waved us on.

"Go girl go," he shouted in a hail of laughter.

And I went, foot to floor. Pushing on to the highway in a blast of horns. Ahead the Holland tunnel. All bright and dazzling and noisy. Eyes scalded by lights. Like a black and white film suddenly turned technicolour. We were stuck in a mega traffic jam surrounded by masses of angry cars jockeying for position as they tried to push their way into the tunnel. Two lanes closed for repair. The cacophony of honking horns drizzled over us like music.

We sighed, clutching each other as if we'd arrived in the promised land or at least discovered The Yellow Brick Road. Lights flooded over us, illuminated my mother's bony face, washed over her liver spotted hands knotted with rosary beads.

I saw in the corner of my eye a gas station. Kim saw it too. She looked at me. We were enveloped in a titter.

My mother's tinny voice quivered over my shoulder. "Wasn't Maebh wonderful. A right little warrior queen."